Edited by Hot Tree Editing

First Published 2026

ISBN 13: 978-1-971653-03-7

One More Face-Off

Shatter the Ice

Book 2

MariaLisa deMora

DEDICATION

"All hockey players are bilingual. They know English and profanity." ~ Gordie Howe

Because hockey makes me happy.

CONTENTS

ACKNOWLEDGMENTS

Watching the 2026 hockey playoffs made me acknowledge something about myself.

I am a hockey addict. Unrepentant.

Some games happened outside of my circadian rhythm and I'd avoid the scoresheet until I had a chance to watch the recording. I don't have any plans on attempting a recovery. I'm not sorry. Could be worse!

I've been lucky enough to have made friends with various players through the years, and if you've never played the game "Sorry" using hockey rules, well, you're missing out!

Because of those friendships, I've had a closer view of the stress the players work under during the season. At the ECHL level, where few players have contracts that can get them a seat at the big show, they're playing for love of the game, not the money, because there just isn't much to go around.

Kinda like my life is now, where the writing is done for myself, for my amusement, and love of the characters. Here's hoping you love Morgan and Marshall as much as I do.

#hockeyfan4life

Woofully yours,
~ML

ONE MORE FACE-OFF

They survived the worst. Now they have to learn how to live.

Morgan Oakson is free. The bruises have faded, the Cup has been lifted, and the man who terrorized him is behind bars. But freedom isn't the same as healing, and love isn't the same as safety.

For Marshall Davies, being part of the team that shepherded the Dingoes to victory was easy. Facing the grave of the sister he couldn't save? Impossible. Fifteen years of buried grief are clawing their way to the surface, and the only person strong enough to hold him together is the same man still learning how to trust again.

Between sold-out arenas, expanding youth clinics, and whispers of forever, Morgan and Marshall must face their deepest scars, together. Because some opponents don't wear jerseys. Some battles aren't won with goals. And sometimes the hardest faceoff isn't on the ice...it's the one against the ghosts you've been running from your whole life.

Emotional, searing, and fiercely romantic, *One More Faceoff* is the breathtaking second chapter in the Shatter the Ice series, where love means showing up, even when it hurts.

CHAPTER ONE

Morgan

Out in the Dingoes' rink, the air thrummed with the electric pulse of the preseason, the first sheet of ice pristine under freshly polished floodlights, its surface catching the arena's glow like a mirror.

Morgan Oakson sat in the locker room, tightening the laces of his skates with deliberate precision, the scent of worn leather and liniment helping him sink into the right headspace, the ritual an island of stability amidst the chaos of his thoughts.

Around him, teammates filled the space with familiar noise and distractions, from Jake's booming laugh cutting through idle chatter, to Riley's quiet focus as he tightened his goalie pads with meticulous care, and Thompson forever tossing a puck between his hands, his lanky frame slouched against a locker.

The championship glow from last season's cup run still lingered, the memory of hoisting the silver trophy vivid in Morgan's mind, its weight a testament to the team's determination and his redemption. But new pressures coiled in his chest, tighter than the laces he pulled taut. He'd been semi-out to most of his teammates since last season, and every day since then, he'd felt exposed, like a player stepping onto the ice without pads, bracing for the inevitable hit of public scrutiny.

He was also trying to balance a real relationship for the first time.

The Dingoes PR manager, Ellis, and Morgan had laid plans for an offseason press release about his sexuality. But every time she'd contacted him, Morgan had begged off because something about the timing didn't feel right.

At every step, as he'd promised to, Marshall had supported his decisions.

And now, here Morgan sat, getting ready for the first unofficial, preseason skate of the returning players. Still in the closet where most of the world was concerned.

He stood, stretching his legs, the locker room's concrete floor solid underneath his skates. His friends' acceptance was a shield forged through late-night confessions and rink-side fist bumps, but the terror of being known, of being really and truly known, was paralyzing.

The legal fight against his ex, Burke Hammond, loomed like a storm cloud, dark and heavy. After Morgan had finally left his abuser for good, Burke'd gone off the rails trying to get his golden goose back. He'd been arrested for breaking and entering and also violating a restraining order. Finally, after months of nothing happening, Burke's court date was set, the upcoming deadline feeling like a ticking bomb.

Whispers of his threats to out Morgan to the media hadn't faded. There'd been so many hatred-filled voicemails, and the worst of them kept replaying in Morgan's mind on a loop.

"You can't hide forever. Pay me now, or you'll lose hockey. Remember me, babe? You owe me."

Nightmares had haunted his sleep all summer, dreams of websites with headlines that screamed "Dingo Star's Secret" and of watching his career crumbling under the weight of exposure. He woke from them feeling off kilter and afraid, and it was irritating that it felt like his own mind was sabotaging him.

I'm stronger now, he reminded himself, Dr. Sanchez's calm voice echoing in his head with her mantra of *"Reclaim your narrative."* but fear gnawed at the edges, sharp and relentless.

Morgan was the first to step on the ice, the rest of the team following closely. He felt the condition of the ice, enjoying how his blades carved smooth arcs, the crisp air biting his cheeks. His mind was heavy, thoughts tangled with courtrooms and cameras. With a mental shake, he brought himself back to the ice, seeing a puck headed his way. Using muscle memory, he snapped a no-look pass to Thompson and found their chemistry as sharp as ever, the puck hitting the tape on his partner's stick with a satisfying thud.

Thompson grinned, returning a quick nod, their silent sync a holdover success from last season's triumphs.

Over the summer, they'd attended the same puck-handling workshop in Toronto where the coaches had to split them up on separate teams because the other players considered their connection an unfair advantage. They'd laughed and bumped fists before skating to their assigned groups.

That week was a good one. Between the company and exhaustion from the workshop, I slept really well. Then there was the weekend spent in the woods with Marshall.

He felt the tips of his ears get hot.

I've slept very well as long as I'm not sleeping alone.

Morgan's eyes flicked to the stands, where Marshall stood, his presence remaining a steady force amidst the uncertainty. It had been about six hours since they'd left Marshall's apartment. After their time in the cabin in the early summer, Morgan had taken to staying over two or three nights a week.

He was still terrified of being outed but was addicted to the affection and attention Marshall lavished on him. He was also addicted to being able to give the same right back to Marshall.

But he can't go out for a meal with me. He's out, left the closet behind him so he could live his truth, and here I am, pulling him back into the closet with me.

Jake skated up and clapped Morgan's shoulder, his grin infectious. "Ready to defend the Cup, superstar?"

Morgan forced a smile, gripping his stick. "Born ready." But as he joined a drill, stickhandling through orange cones with precision, his mom's hesitant voice from their phone conversation still rang in his ears. *"I'll try, honey,"* she'd said, her love tangled with worry. He hadn't spoken to her since, hoping if he left it to her, she'd reach out.

She hadn't.

He was also all up in his head with anything associated with Burke, remembering each detail threw a dark shadow over everything. Sometimes the ice felt both safe and precarious, a tightrope between his past and the battles ahead.

He pushed harder, weaving through the cones, each turn in defiance of fear, a vow to hold his ground.

The mostly performative skate ended with a whistle, and players made their way off the ice, their shouts fading. Morgan lingered on the bench, catching his breath, the Zamboni's quiet hum settling his nerves as it crunched onto the ice out of the tunnel. He glanced at Marshall again, their eyes meeting, a spark of hope cutting through the weight.

The season stretched ahead, filled with games and courtroom dates, the threat of his truth laid bare.

Gripping his stick, resolve hardened like ice under pressure.

I've faced worse. I'll face this.

The rink gleamed again, the Zamboni leaving it a blank slate for battles new and old.

* * *

Marshall

Marshall leaned against the cool glass of the management box, the Dingoes' rink sprawling below, its ice a gleaming stage under the arena's stark lights. Players' blades hissed, their shouts and stick taps bouncing off the cavernous walls, a symphony of grit and focus.

Morgan wove through a drill, his pivots quick, passes to Thompson crisp, a far cry from the haunted man Marshall remembered from last year's season with the Geese. It had only been after Marshall had arranged a trade with the Dingoes that he'd gotten to see Morgan enjoy hockey again. A warm pulse of pride flooded through Marshall's chest, but anxiety gnawed beneath it. Their cautious beginning of a relationship would have to remain a secret tethered to the professional boundaries he couldn't breach.

They'd had many conversations during the offseason, as well as intimate moments because attempting to bank the heat didn't mean it ever went away.

As GM, his role demanded impartiality, a line he held with care, but Morgan's tense shoulders, the way his gaze darted to the stands, stirred a protective urge Marshall fought to temper.

He picked up his clipboard from a nearby table. The front paper was dense with the list of incoming team players' names inked in his precise handwriting. He let the coach manage the lines, but as GM, Marshall worked hand in hand with him when it came to picking up new players.

Today they'd had fifteen returning players, including Thompson, Jake, Riley, and Antoly. One player who hadn't returned, deciding instead to retire a Cup winner, was Greer. The loss of the team's captain would be addressed before the first regulation game. Another thing that sat firmly in the coach's hands, and he'd been pleased when Masterson had indicated he'd take account of player feedback. Marshall watched Morgan playing in sync with Thompson, their seamless chemistry a cornerstone of the team's defensive lines.

Marshall tapped the page with his pen, his mind drifting to stolen moments from over the summer. He'd made a promise to himself as he stole a sweet kiss with

Morgan's hand still brushing his. He would continue supporting and loving Morgan, no matter what.

He's carrying enough without me complicating things, he thought.

A memory burst into his mind, his own team captain the cause of his sister's bruises. Through it all, his sister had battled quietly against her abuser. He remembered her tightly balled fists, her resolve to reclaim her life. *Unsuccessful. It had still been stolen from her.*

Keeping his and Morgan's love hidden felt like a betrayal, yet it was a necessary evil. Morgan needed stability, and Marshall's duties demanded focus.

His phone buzzed, Ellis's name lighting the screen. "Hey, boss. Interestingly enough, the league is pushing a diversity initiative this season," she said when he answered, her voice brisk but warm. "Panel discussions. Maybe a campaign. It could be a platform for Morgan if he's ready to go public. He's been so hesitant all summer, running hot and cold about the plans we'd made. This might be the path to get him to better emotional health. Thoughts?"

Marshall's gaze flicked to Morgan, now joking with Jake at the bench, his smile bright but fleeting, a mask that couldn't fully hide the strain of Burke's upcoming trial. Ellis's idea had promise, allowing Marshall and the team to support Morgan's truth without forcing it, amplifying his significant strength for the benefit of the league. "Sounds promising," Marshall replied, voice measured. "But it's his call. He's got enough on his plate with the legal aspects looming."

"I'm aware of the trial. We're working with Morgan's legal team on all of this too. If he comes out before the trial and can talk about the blackmail Hammond forced on him, that might be better for the case." She sighed. "I'll refine the plan. This one is officially Plan N, just so you know." She laughed. "I'll keep plugging away."

"Thanks," Marshall chuckled. "We'll both talk to Morgan about the idea. Let me know when you're ready."

"Will do," Ellis promised, her tone confident.

Marshall watched Morgan skate, his form fluid despite the mental weight he carried. The season would be a balancing act between leadership, love, and looming threats. A text from Ellis buzzed again, *Media plan N ready for preseason coming-out. His call.*

Marshall exhaled, knowing Morgan's choice could reshape everything, their love tested by the spotlight. As practice wound down, Morgan glanced up, their eyes locking through the glass, a jolt of hope tangled with restraint. Marshall vowed to walk the line carefully. For Morgan's sake and his own.

***

Morgan

The hallway was dim, his post-skate buzz slowly fading as Morgan lingered near the exit, his personal gear bag heavy on his shoulder. The air carried the sharp chill of the arena, the cooling system's low hum a steady drone.

Their first chance for the returning players to skate together had been solid, but tension simmered inside him. *I swear I'm just worried about Burke.*

Marshall appeared, walking over from the management wing, his broad frame filling the narrow space, their cautious connection a quiet echo of a past moment. Morgan still remembered their first stolen kiss in a shadowed alcove.

"Hey," Marshall said, voice low, eyes searching. "You were electric out there. You okay, though? Look tense."

Morgan shifted, the bag's strap digging into his shoulder, the ache a reminder of his resolve. "Game's fine. It's Burke. The idea of the legal mess, with all the media sniffing around pre-season, and his threats to out me. I'm holding it together, but it's heavy." His voice carried an edge, but he attempted to soften it, meeting Marshall's gaze. "You looked good in that GM suit." He eyed Marshall's clothing. "Why the wardrobe change?"

"Yeah, I'm heading over to the YMCA. Tonight is my turn to supervise the LGBTQ+ kids until around ten o'clock. I've found the suit doesn't work well with the kids."

"I forgot that was tonight. Good luck. I had such a blast working with Cambell's foundation during the offseason. Love that he's bringing hockey to kids who are disadvantaged. Wrangling an even dozen twelve-year-olds who all wanted to learn was hard enough." Morgan grinned. He lowered his voice and said, "And, just for the record, I think you look good in the polo and jeans too."

Marshall shoved his hands into the front pockets of his jeans, restraint clear in every line of his body. "God, Morgan. You make it hard to remember our agreement. We'll still keep it tight in public, for the team, for you. And yes, for me. I know we've got lots and lots of reasons for the agreement, but it's not easy."

Their eyes locked, the air charged with unspoken heat, but Morgan stepped back, needing distance to stay focused. "Yeah, I know."

Marshall made the next move, slipping to the side and passing Morgan in the hallway. "I've got to go now so I'm on time at the Y." Marshall paused, turning to look at Morgan. "Also for the record, from my perspective, you look good in everything."

Marshall lingered, the hallway's dim light casting soft shadows on their faces. The air between them felt charged, the faint chill seeping through the walls. Morgan stepped closer, not quite touching, but close enough to feel the warmth radiating from Marshall's body.

"You know, those kids at the Y? They remind me of you sometimes," Marshall said, voice quiet, eyes searching Morgan's. "Scared, but tough. Like how you were last season, pushing through."

Morgan's chest tightened at the vulnerability Marshall had observed that echoed his own fears from the preseason jitters.

He said, "I really think working with Campbell's foundation over the summer helped. Seeing those kids who'd never even thought about hockey before, league hockey too out of reach, and then getting to watch them light up on the ice reminds me why I'm doing this." He hesitated, then added softly, "Why I'm ready to face whatever comes with Burke. Every time I start feeling too scared, I remember those kids."

Marshall nodded, reaching out to squeeze Morgan's shoulder, lingering just a moment, the contact firm and reassurin. Their foreheads nearly touched, breaths mingling in the quiet space. "You're stronger than you know, Morgan. We've might have public boundaries, but I'm here. Discreetly, like we agreed. And you know my door is always open for you." The touch sent a familiar spark through Morgan, a reminder of their promise to keep their connection to a slow-burn in public , but he craved the *more* they'd found through the summer, which now made pulling back harder every day.

Morgan exhaled, stepping away with effort. "Thanks. It means a lot. More than you know."

Marshall gave him a small smile and headed out as Morgan leaned against the wall, the public distance necessary even as it made his heart ache, leaving him craving closeness with Marshall.

Might need to negotiate our agreement again. Maybe I'll be waiting in the apartment when he gets home tonight.

He headed to the parking lot. The night air was cool, and brilliant stars pierced the dark like pinpricks.

A figure lingered by a nearby car. They were tall, shadowed, and the silhouette looked way too familiar. *Burke?* Panic spiked, Burke's threats flashing through his mind. *"I'll ruin you."*

Morgan froze, breath catching, then shook it off, climbing into his truck, resolve hardening. He gripped the wheel, the engine's rumble steadying him, making him more determined to face the season's battles.

***

Marshall

Marshall held his breath as he walked away from Morgan, the hallway's dim light casting everything in sharp relief. A glance over his shoulder showed him Morgan's silhouette sharp against the background. He was carrying a weight Marshall couldn't ease.

The memory of their private embraces burned, but their mutual insistence on professionalism was the only way to go, aligning with Marshall's own boundaries as GM. Pride in Morgan clashed with worry. Hammond's trial and the potential media exposure were closing in, a storm Marshall couldn't shield him from entirely. He wanted to go back, to comfort Morgan, but he held back, his role clear.

Lingering in his running car, Marshall checked his phone. Ellis had already sent him new notes on the diversity initiative, a plan to amplify Morgan's courage if he chose to go public. A glance out the window showed him that Morgan had paused in the lot, staring at a figure by a car. Marshall's gut twisted. *Was it Hammond?* Couldn't be. *Maybe it's someone tied to Hammond's circle?* That possibility sent a chill down his spine. He texted the security chief with a brief, *Check video of player lot security. Possible issue timestamped now. Send copies to me, Coach, and Ellis.*

Morgan finally drove off, the taillights fading. The man, whether or not he'd been a potential threat, had disappeared into the shadows. Marshall exhaled, hating that his and Morgan's fragile pledge could be tested by shadows old and new.

The season loomed, a test of love and duty, and Marshall steeled himself to protect Morgan, no matter the cost.

***

Morgan

Morgan was frozen in the arena parking lot, the October chill slicing through his thin jacket, seeping into his bones as he gripped his car keys, their cold, jagged edges biting into his palm. The floodlights cast stark, elongated shadows across the cracked asphalt, turning every parked car into a potential hiding place.

The distant hum of traffic along the suburban highway barely registered over the thunder of his heartbeat, a relentless drum that drowned out the world. The figure he'd glimpsed after practice—tall, shadowed, and way too familiar—was no trick of the mind. Burke's cologne, a sharp, suffocating blend of cedar and musk, hit him like a physical blow, dragging him back to the terror of their shared past: Burke's iron grip on his wrist, the hissed threats in their dimly lit apartment. "You're mine, Morgan. Always." The memory was visceral, a ghost that clawed at his senses, pulling him into a spiral of fear.

As he woke, his breath was ragged and shallow. His anxiety surged, a tidal wave crashing through his chest.

He could still feel the phantom ache of fractured ribs, the air stolen from his lungs by Burke's fists in those early, desperate days when he couldn't understand what his life had turned into and escape seemed impossible.

The dream was gone now, melted into the dark corners of his mind, but the memory of the cologne lingered, seemingly tangible, a real and suffocating presence that clung to the air like damp fog.

Regretting having come back to his own apartment last night, he swung his legs over the edge of the bed, but when he went to stand, his knees buckled slightly, leaving him crouched beside his bed, bracing himself on the frame as if it were a shield. His fingers trembled as he fumbled for his phone. The screen's glow felt too bright, exposing him, but he hit the autodial button set up for Marshall, the ringing in his ear an anchor to reality.

"Morgan? Is everything okay?"

"Earlier, I should have called earlier. But I thought I had to be wrong."

"Morgan, tell me what's wrong."

He whispered, voice tight, barely audible over the pulse roaring in his ears. "Burke. He might be out on bail. I think I saw him outside the arena, maybe even smelled his cologne. If I did, he would violate the restraining order again. But I don't know if it was him." His words stumbled, each one fighting against the panic squeezing his throat. He scanned the room, eyes darting to every shadow, each flicker of movement a potential threat, Burke's silhouette lurked in his imagination. His tight grip had the phone digging deeper into his palm, keeping him in the moment.

I'm safe here. Safe with Marshall. Safe.

Marshall's voice cut through, calm and measured, a beacon in the storm. "You're home now, right? Stay safe. I'm right here. You're not alone." He nodded, though Marshall couldn't see, grabbing hold of the hope the words gave him. Like a lifeline to someone tossed into churning waters.

Morgan climbed to his feet and rushed to the door. It was locked already, but he took a moment to unlock and relock the door. He threw the deadbolt home with a heavy click, the sound a small victory against the fear.

"Yeah, I'm safe. The door is locked." Morgan slumped against the door, sliding to the floor. "Maybe it was just a dream? Nothing seems real right now."

"It's okay, Morgan. What do you remember?"

The low growl of Marshall's voice steadied him, but he couldn't get away from the memory of Burke.

I'm not that broken man anymore, he told himself, Dr. Sanchez's lessons echoing through to today. *I'm safe, and I will reclaim my strength and own my narrative.* But Burke's shadow loomed, a specter testing his resolve even as he navigated his memories, heart still racing, the night a maze of threats he couldn't outrun.

"I don't know. There was a guy. Maybe. I'm beginning to I think I imagined it." He shook his head. "I drove home. Nothing was wrong when I got here. Nothing's wrong now." He pulled in a shaky breath. "I think I imagined it."

"No, I saw the man at the parking garage too. I've already messaged the security chief to get the video from the lot. He'll have that tonight, if I know him at all. I can forward a copy to Gary. You didn't imagine a strange person in the parking garage. Can you wait until tomorrow? You're safe right now, and you'll stay there, safe."

"You saw someone too? Why didn't you tell me?"

"Morgan, I am telling you. You left, no one followed you out of the parking garage. I initiated a investigation with someone I trust. And then I went to the YMCA because by then I was in danger of being late for the kids."

He could hear frustration in Marshall's voice for maybe the first time. Morgan ran that timeline back through his head, knuckles white as his hands clutched at each other. His apartment was usually a refuge, but after the dream, the hallway seemed to stretch on endlessly.

"What are you thinking right now, Morgan?" Marshall's tone of command pulled Morgan out of his head.

"I'm thinking that you wouldn't have let me leave if you didn't believe I was safe. I'm thinking I need to trust you to have my back." He sucked in a hard breath. "You've got my back, Marshall. You've got my back."

"I do, Morgan. I always will. I can be your refuge in all of this. I will be the person you can trust to have your back because I do."

Morgan's phone buzzed in his hand, and he jumped as if shot. He pulled it away from his ear to see a text from Jake. *Yo, you good? Missed you at post-practice beers.*

Morgan exhaled, the team's warmth a faint light in the dark. He didn't reply, not yet, his focus on Marshall. The apartment felt safer somehow, Marshall's presence on the phone a promise of security.

"I'm good now." It was partly a lie, but one Morgan had been telling himself for a long time. He pushed to his feet, scanning the shadows in the apartment one last time before checking the lock on the door again, his resolve fragile but growing.

***

"No, Ellis. This doesn't feel like the best time. You know, it doesn't feel good."

A low feminine sigh came through the phone. He was testing her last nerve, and he knew it.

"I'm sorry."

"No, don't be sorry. But let me talk through a couple of things. Indulge me. Hear me out before you say no."

"Okay. I'm game."

Ellis pulled in an audible breath. Morgan knew this wasn't going to end like the rest of their calls had. "I'm always playing the 'what-if' game, when it comes to the press. You know that. We've engaged in a few conversations like that."

He nodded, even though she couldn't see him. "Yeah, it's a good exercise."

"Okay, this is just 'what if,' but what if Burke manages to out you during the hearings? We have been able to keep your association with him quiet so far, but as the trial for his breaking and entering comes closer, I fear it's only a matter of time before an astute reporter looks up to see if the Morgan Oakson listed as a plaintiff is the same one who's a hockey player. Then what happens? There's public testimony that you lived together because that's how the B and E stuck. You'd ended the lease, informed him, and he still went back." She went quiet for a moment. "Breathe, Morgan, you're going to pass out if you don't."

He sucked in a lungful of air, then a second one. "That's my worst fear, right there. An enterprising reporter coming up to me with a threat so they can get dibs on the story."

"It's a possibility. We've been lucky so far. Your close circle all knows, right?"

"Yeah, Jake, Thompson, Riley, Antoly. I told Greer, too, but he's no longer in a position to let something escape, or at least it's less likely to be from him."

"Do you trust those men?"

"Well, yeah. They wouldn't do anything to hurt me. Not on purpose."

"So you've heard my fears. Those 'what-if' concepts are what haunt my dreams."

Morgan hung his head. "I know I'm not the only one carrying the burden of planning. I know I've thrown monkey wrenches in each of your plans, all through the summer. I don't know what to do."

"Whatever we do, we're going to do it together because you're not alone. Together we'll find the right time and place for your truth, Morgan. But you gotta trust me at some point."

"I do trust you, Ellis. It's the rest of the world that scares the shit out of me."

CHAPTER TWO

Morgan

The suburban bar glowed with a gritty warmth, neon signs buzzing over weathered wooden booths, their red-and-blue flickers casting a soft haze across the room. The clink of beer glasses and bursts of raucous laughter sliced through the smoky air, mingling with the jukebox's thump, the raw chords of the current song a pulse that matched the Dingoes' post-practice energy.

Morgan sat wedged between Jake and Riley at a long table, its weathered top scratched with a hundred scars. Wings and pitchers were scattered amidst crumpled napkins and half-empty ketchup bottles. He nursed a soda, the fizz sharp and cold against his tongue, a stark contrast to the turmoil still churning from the mysterious stranger's presence in the lot a week ago.

His hands were hidden under the table, but he could still feel them trembling slightly. The memory of that dream, complete with scents of cedar and musk, lingered like a bad memory. But the team's easy camaraderie was a relief, his circle of friends pulling him back from the edge.

Jake leaned forward, his broad frame spilling over the booth as he wiped buffalo sauce from his chin with a napkin, his grin wide and unyielding. "All right, boys, here's a big idea," he said, voice cutting through the bar's din. "Riley and me were talking. What if we suggest a queer-friendly charity game, one where we can raise funds earmarked for different inclusion programs. Morgan, you inspired it, man, with your truth." He clapped Morgan's shoulder, the gesture heavy with the same loyalty that had steadied him through late-night talks when Morgan first bared his soul. The touch was a necessary reminder that he wasn't alone even as Burke's shadow loomed.

Riley nodded, relaxed in a faded hoodie, his hands steady despite the chaos around them. "Yeah, we thought we could pitch the idea to Coach and then the league. Make it a big thing. Show the world that Dingoes stand for something. What do you think? You in?" His eyes met Morgan's, calm but expectant, offering a space to step forwards without pressure.

Morgan's throat tightened. The reality of making his announcement was becoming clear, leaving his gut twisting. He'd suffered more than a year of weekly threats to out him, a plan Burke would recount in great detail at every opportunity, chortling over his ability to ruin Morgan.

The team's faith in him and their unyielding support bolstered him, a warmth that cut through the chill. He'd been a late-season addition to their ranks last year, but the fit had turned out to be incredible. Everything they gave him, he wanted to give it back doubled. *And that starts right now.*

"I…yeah, I'm in. I'd be in," he said, his voice growing more steady with each word, becoming firmer as he leaned into their trust. "Just…gotta keep it low-key for now, with the trial." He glanced at Thompson, slouched across the table, his lanky frame loose but attentive, a fry dangling from his fingers as he gave a thumbs-up.

"Low-key but loud where it counts," Thompson said, tossing the fry with a smirk. "We got you, Oakson. Always."

His casual ease, paired with the other men's nods, sparked a fire in Morgan, a defiance against the fear that clung to him. "Know what? Ellis has a hundred plans for how I can come out to the world, but maybe a charity game is the right vibe. I'll have to ask her, but it's a thought."

The table erupted in agreement, drinks raised, the clink of glass on glass a vow that drowned out the jukebox's wail.

"To the Dingoes!" Jake roared, and laughter followed.

The bar's warmth wrapped around Morgan like a shield. He joined the planning, his voice growing stronger as he suggested a youth hockey clinic tie-in, picturing kids, scared and hiding like he once was, and giving them a chance to find a place on the ice.

"Let's get local queer youth groups involved," he said, the idea sparking in his mind, a way to give back what the team had given him.

Riley jotted it down, nodding, while Jake sketched a rough timeline on a napkin, sauce smudging the ink.

"The GM volunteers at a local YMCA with a LGBTQ+ group of kids," Morgan told them. "We should loop him in on the idea before we go too far down the road. Maybe when I talk to Ellis."

"Aww, they'll be joy killers." Thompson pouted. "But fine, we'll let the adults in on the fun."

The conversation flowed as they talked about potential sponsorships, jersey designs, a fan meet-and-greet, each idea knitting their little group tighter, pushing Morgan's fear just a little farther down the road.

He sipped his soda and let himself laugh at Thompson's terrible pun about "icing" the competition. The fear didn't vanish, but it shrank, dwarfed by his friends' unwavering support, their voices a chorus that carried him forward.

***

Morgan sat stiffly on the couch in his apartment, the room's soft amber walls and spartan furniture still a stark echo of his desperate escape months ago, when fear of Burke's fists kept him awake, heart pounding in the dark. The lamp's dim glow cast long shadows across the floor, and he could hear the faint hum of traffic outside, a distant reminder of the world beyond these walls.

His phone rested heavy in his hand, the most recent call from Gary at the forefront of his mind. He shook off the memories of nights of hiding from Burke and the days of hiding who he was. *I'm not that guy anymore.* He felt stronger now, no longer the terrified man expecting Burke's shadow at every turn.

The security chief had called with the information from the parking garage video a while back. Morgan checked his phone. More than two hours ago, and here he was, still frozen on the couch.

He hit the autodial number and waited for the call to connect, wincing when it rolled over to voicemail. "Hey. It's me. I...uh, would you come over? If you can. If you can't, that's okay. Sorry to bother. It's just that Burke was there, outside the arena," Morgan said, voice low, repeating what Gary had told him earlier. He traced the card's worn edges, its texture a tether to the present. "It's like he's still trying to control me, even on bail. I'm scared he'll out me before I'm ready and ruin everything for me. My hockey and the team." The words spilled out, raw and heavy, but saying them felt like loosening a knot, easing the chokehold of fear. "He was there. Would you come over?"

He hung up and immediately dialed Dr. Sanchez's service, scheduling an emergency session for later in the day. *At least I'll talk to her before dark.*

She called less than ten minutes later, and he let Dr. Sanchez's calm pull him back from the edge.

"I thought I saw Burke the other day, after an unofficial practice. Even the media didn't know we were going to be at the stadium that day. He was in the parking garage. I hoped it wasn't him, but Gary confirmed it earlier today. He's on security footage, standing in the shadows for nearly two hours until he saw me. Then he spent only seconds visible, making sure I saw him." He pulled in a hard breath. "What kind of crazy person waits more than two hours to try and scare another human?"

"You're not that man he controlled, Morgan. You escaped, built a life, and have a great group of friends. Focus on that strength you share with your teammates, your GM, and me. What's one thing you can hold onto tonight?" Her words were a reminder of the progress he'd fought for, the battles won in therapy and on the ice.

Morgan exhaled, long and slow, his breath steadying as he thought of the bar's warmth, Riley's quiet nod, and Thompson's tossed fry. "My team," he said, voice firmer. "They're planning this charity game, for me, for others like me. It's solid. Real." The words reminded him of vulnerability that was no longer a weakness but a bridge to his allies, a strength he hadn't known he possessed. He pictured the bar's neon glow, the raised glasses, the laughter that was always successful in drowning out Burke's words, and he felt a spark of defiance kindle in his chest.

"Good," Dr. Sanchez said, her tone warm. "Hold that close. Did Gary mention the police? Remember, you're not alone in this."

"He did, but they hadn't even told us that Burke had gotten bail. Gary's going to find a better lawyer for me. At least they know he was here." The assurance settled over him, a barrier against the night's threats. "Thank you for helping me, Dr. Sanchez."

"It is my absolute pleasure, Morgan. Call back if things get sideways again."

Twenty minutes later, a soft knock echoed through the apartment. Morgan peered through the peephole, relief flooding him at Marshall's familiar frame. He opened the door, and Marshall stepped in, holding two steaming coffees, his expression a mix of concern and restraint.

"I figured you could use this," Marshall said, holding out a cup. "Black, no sugar. And so we're clear, this is me putting my boyfriend hat on, not the GM one."

Morgan let out a deep breath, feeling tension flow from his muscles. "Hi." He took both cups of coffee and set them to the side. "You have no idea how much I needed this."

Leaning in, he wrapped his arms around Marshall and settled against his firm, sturdy body. Marshall's arms came around Morgan, and it was like time stopped, peace flowing in to drown out the fears.

Thirty minutes later, they were sharing a corner at his small kitchen table, the creak of chairs and the faint hum of traffic outside filling the room.

Morgan wrapped his hands around his cup of coffee, the lukewarm heat seeping into his chilled fingers. "My dreams have been so bad. The memories in them hit like a punch. Keep pulling me right back to nights I spent hiding, back when I was a bruised and scared kid. My dad's voice still in my head, telling me I'm weak for not being 'man enough.'"

Marshall's eyes softened, and he reached across the table, covering Morgan's hand with his own. He shifted closer, their knees bumping under the table. "You're not weak. You shouldn't doubt yourself. You've got to keep going, just like you are now. Calling me had to be hard, but I'm glad you did."

"I needed to hear the truth," Morgan told him. "I knew I could count on you to do whatever was best for me. It's been a lot. Seeing Burke, facing preseason with all this hanging over me? Makes me feel weak, but around you,

I feel like I could do anything." He angled in slightly, turning his hand to thread their fingers together.

They held hands for a moment, then Marshall shifted so his thumb rubbed slow circles over the back of his hand. The touch was comforting, nondemanding, and Marshall's scent, composed entirely of clean soap and rink chill, was a stark contrast to Burke's ghost.

Morgan wanted to lean into it, so he went with his gut feeling and rested his head on Marshall's shoulder, inhaling deeply. "I feel so much stronger, but all of this shook me."

They pulled apart slowly, Marshall's hand lingering on Morgan's arm, stroking lightly before dropping away.

"I'm glad you came, Marshall. Real glad. Thank you. I know you've got a thousand things to do before the season opens. You don't have to stay here. I'm good now."

Marshall nodded, blew out a breath, then stood. "Okay. You wanna come back to mine? Want me to stay the night?" He brushed his hand across the back of Morgan's neck.

"No, I'm okay now. Rational understanding and all that. I've got you on speed dial. If I need to hear your voice, I'll call."

"Okay. You better." Marshall bent over, and Morgan lifted his chin. The kiss was warm and comforting,

Marshall's lips tasting of sweet coffee and affection. The caress ended gradually, both men pulling away slowly. "If you don't want me to stay the night, I need to get going. Morgan, be sure to get some rest and remember that you are not alone." He left after a final kiss, the door clicking shut, but the warmth of his touch lingered, guarding Morgan against the fear.

Morgan locked the door and then went to the bedroom to sit on the side of the bed, the creak of the springs a familiar sound. He was vulnerable, yes, but defiant, the team's support reassuring, the ice waiting for him to reclaim his game.

He closed his eyes, the apartment no longer a prison but a stepping stone, and resolved to face Burke's shadow and the season ahead.

He stood, pacing through the apartment, the idea of the charity game bouncing around in his mind. It would be a chance to turn his fear into something tangible and good. He pictured kids in the stands, queer youth like he'd been, scared but dreaming of the ice. He thought of the team's plan, their laughter, their raised glasses of solidarity. He knew they were pushing because he needed them to, helping him create a legacy that didn't include Burke.

His phone buzzed again, a text from Jake. *Clinic idea is really good, man. Especially tied to the charity game. You're killing it.*

Morgan smiled, the weight of the night easing. He quickly responded to Jake, giving him the details of a couple more ideas he'd had. He wasn't alone. Not anymore. The apartment felt less oppressive, the remaining traces of Marshall's scent lifting the mood.

What we have is real. It's not just about a quick release—never has been. We're building something between us that's larger than even my imagination.

He sat again, resolve hardening. He was ready to face the ice, the trial, and whatever Burke threw next, with his team, and his Marshall, behind him.

***

Marshall

Marshall's feet sank into the plush carpet in a sleek league office, the conference table polished to a mirror shine, city skyline glinting through floor-to-ceiling windows. League officials in crisp suits flipped through his proposal of anti-harassment policies and wellness programs, all inspired by the diversity initiative Ellis had mentioned. Morgan's courage drove him, the memory of his rink-side promise burning bright. As GM, he could push for safer, more inclusive spaces, not just for the Dingoes, but league wide.

"These policies help protect players' mental health," Marshall said, voice steady, hands folded to hide his nerves. "Harassment, on or off the ice, undermines performance. We all know that. It's why rookie hazing hasn't been part of hockey for decades. Like everything else in the world, things in the hockey world also keep changing. Now we need clear reporting channels and strong support systems."

The officials nodded, one jotting notes, the idea clearly gaining traction. Morgan's fight, though unspoken, was the heartbeat of his pitch, a vow to shield him and others.

Back at his hotel, the night quiet except for a distant siren, Marshall called Morgan, the phone's soft buzz a reprieve. "Hey, how are you holding up?"

Morgan's voice was tired but warm. "It's not easy yet, if that's what you're asking." He chuckled. "Everything is still swirling around in my skull. Thanks for checking in."

"Always," Marshall said, a smile tugging at his lips. The call lingered, intimate in its restraint, their connection a steady pulse beneath the professional surface. "You're doing more than you know, Morgan. Keep going." He paused and lowered his voice to ask, "Are you at the apartment?"

"Yeah," Morgan said with a laugh. "I miss you here, but I tried to go back to my place, and I missed you like crazy, so I came back here."

"I don't mind. I like knowing you're in our bed."

"In our bed," Morgan echoed. "I like it too."

When they finally hung up, Marshall stared out the window, the city lights blurring, his advocacy and their bond intertwined, a foundation for battles ahead.

CHAPTER THREE

Morgan

Morgan sat rigid in the courtroom, the sterile air heavy with tension and fear. Echoing footsteps of clerks and the rustle of legal papers disturbed the silence, amplifying the knot in his stomach. There were no jurors. The judge's bench, the sole source of decision over the outcome, loomed large over the room.

Morgan's lawyers sat as a stark barrier between him and Burke, who was across the way, his glare cutting through the space like a blade. Morgan's pulse raced, every bad memory of Burke's fists bruising his ribs and of being pinned by him in their old apartment were vivid today. This hearing was about Burke's most recent restraining order violation.

When called to testify, Morgan walked to the witness stand and took a seat, smoothing his tie. When he spoke, his voice steady despite the tremor in his hands. "He was there, outside where I work, close enough I could identify his cologne. It's an expensive one that smells like cedar and musk. This was the first time I've seen him, but he's ignored the order before and left a bunch of voicemails demanding money." The words spilled out, each one a step away from the fear that once silenced him.

Burke's lips curled, and as Morgan returned to his seat, a whispered threat reached him: "You'll regret this,

Morgan." The words slithered, cold and familiar, but Morgan met his gaze, defiance burning in his gut.

The judge's gavel cracked, voice firm. "Mr. Tolly, remind your client that threatening the plaintiff in my court will not be tolerated. I'm ordering the restraining order extended, no contact, and am also ordering closely monitored bail conditions. Let's check in twice a week to his assigned officer."

Relief flooded Morgan, but Burke's stare lingered, a shadow that followed him out into the courthouse hall, where Gary waited.

He clasped Morgan's shoulder for a moment, the strength of his grip a reminder that he wasn't alone. "I gotta go, but you did good, kiddo."

Morgan nodded, the victory bittersweet. Burke's whisper echoed as he stepped into the daylight, and his resolve hardened, but unease still clung to him like damp clothes.

As agreed, Marshall waited on the sidewalk, his GM suit again traded for a casual polo. He scanned Morgan with quiet concern. "You okay?"

He shook his head, and with Marshall's hand underneath his elbow, they moved quickly across the street to a backroom in a nearby diner Marshall had arranged, the quiet space offering privacy for Morgan to recover his composure.

Morgan leaned against the wall, exhaling shakily. "Did you hear? Did Gary call you? He whispered a threat, right there in the courtroom. Another poisonous version of 'You'll regret this.' It hit hard, echoed around like he's still in my head. But the fact that the judge heard him? That's a definite win. He didn't hesitate to order an extension. I think it's all a win."

"Gary called, yes. We both care about you. You've got so many people in your corner, Morgan. And Hammond is a prick, but he seems to be a stupid prick, pulling that in the actual courtroom."

Morgan felt a grin begin to spread his lips, and relief washed over him, the weight he'd carried for so long lifted a bit, and he closed the distance, glad of the privacy as he cupped Marshall's face and pulled him down into a kiss.

It grew, becoming both deeper and sweeter, their lips parting, tongues brushing in a slow, heated exploration that tasted of so many hard-won victories. Marshall's hands framed Morgan's waist, drawing him closer, the solid press of their bodies igniting a spark that echoed every encounter they'd had through the months.

Morgan broke it first, breath ragged, their foreheads touching. "I feel so much closer to whole, Marshall. Like I can finally breathe without looking over my shoulder. At least a little bit."

Marshall's thumb traced Morgan's jaw, his eyes dark with want but tempered by restraint. "You are whole. I'm proud."

"I can't risk the team, or risk their trust and loyalty." Morgan shook his head. "But I'm not going to be so afraid, I risk losing you. We're in this."

They kissed again, Morgan's arms finding their way around Marshall's neck as he stretched up the scant inches that separated them. Marshall was the first to pull back this time, breathing as labored as Morgan's. He stared into Marshall's eyes, seeing the want and trust there. The kiss lingered in the air, a turning point, before Marshall stepped back, honoring their agreement.

Morgan hesitated, then reached out and stopped Marshall. "Can I go with you? I don't want to be alone."

"Of course," Marshall said, gripping Morgan's hand for a moment. "Let's go."

***

Marshall

The apartment belonged to Marshall and looked like it.

A stylish brick third-floor walk-up on the edge of the city's old mill district, it had one bedroom, one bath, and windows tall enough to let the streetlights paint gold ladders across the hardwood at night.

The place smelled of pine from a bookshelf he'd refinished last summer, the scent reminding Marshall of lazy days and sweet nights. There was also the aroma of coffee that never quite dissipated, and now, a new citrus shampoo joined in the mix, drifting from the bathroom where Morgan had just showered.

His lover stood at the kitchen counter, slicing apples, the knife flashing silver under the pendant lamp. He wore one of Marshall's Henleys, this one gray with sleeves shoved to the elbows, the hem skimming the tops of his thighs. No pants. The sight had become familiar in the past months, but it still stole Marshall's breath every time he came home from the rink and found Morgan like this, bare-legged, humming something tuneless, the city's distant sirens and horns a soft counterpoint.

Marshall dropped his keys into the bowl by the door. It felt good to shed the isolating GM persona, one layer at a time. He toed off his shoes and lined them up beside Morgan's scuffed sneakers. The domesticity of it made his chest tight in the best way.

"Hey, stranger," Morgan said without turning, the knife paused mid-slice. "You're late."

"Traffic on the bridge," Marshall lied. Truth was, he'd stopped at the corner market for the honey Morgan liked, the kind with the comb still inside. He placed the paper bag on the counter. "Brought you something."

Morgan glanced over his shoulder, eyes lighting at the label on the bag. "You remembered."

"Hard to forget the way you moan when you eat it." Marshall's voice was gravel and affection. He took the glass jar out of the bag and set it down carefully.

Morgan's cheeks pinked. He abandoned the apples, wiped his hands on a dishtowel, and crossed the small kitchen in three steps. Marshall met him halfway, hands settling low on Morgan's hips, thumbs brushing the strip of belly exposed as he pulled the Henley up. Morgan rose on tiptoe, kissed him hello, a sweet caress that was soft, lingering, tasting of green apple and want.

They had learned this language in the cabin, the way Morgan's breath caught when Marshall's beard scraped his throat, how Marshall's fingers flexed against Morgan's hips when he was trying not to rush. Here, in the city, the grammar had only grown richer.

Morgan pulled back just enough to rest his forehead against Marshall's. "Shower first," he murmured. "You smell like contracts, bad decisions, and—" he inhaled, "—man."

Marshall chuckled. "That a complaint?"

"It's a promise," Morgan said and tugged him towards the bedroom.

The bathroom was decent sized, subway tile patterns meeting in the corners, the shower plenty big for the two of them. According to Morgan, they made it work really well.

Marshall stripped efficiently, suit jacket first, then all the bits in between, and finally boxer briefs, all while Morgan watched from the doorway, arms folded, lip caught between his teeth. When Marshall stepped under the spray, Morgan followed, still in the Henley until the water plastered it to his skin, turning the gray fabric sheer.

"Off," Marshall said, voice low. "Off now." He hooked his fingers under the hem and peeled it upward.

Morgan lifted his arms, then let the shirt drop with a wet slap onto the tile. Water streamed over his shoulders, tracing the faint scars from a hundred slashes across his ribs and the constellation of freckles on his chest that Marshall had memorized with his mouth.

They didn't speak. Words felt clumsy under the hiss of water. Instead, Marshall reached for the soap and worked it between his palms until suds bloomed. He started at Morgan's neck, thumbs pressing into the knots there, then down the slope of his shoulders, the lean muscle of his arms. Morgan's head fell back, his eyes closed, lips parted on a silent sigh. Marshall's hands moved lower, grazing Morgan's chest, his nipples pebbling under his thumbs and belly giving softly as Marshall kept going. When he reached Morgan's cock, half hard and flushed, he didn't linger, just washed him, gentle, reverent, then turned him to rinse.

Morgan braced his hands on the tile, water cascading down his spine. Marshall pushed against him from behind, chest to back, cock nestling between the cheeks of Morgan's ass. Not hurrying, just there, a warm weight. He wrapped soap-slick arms around Morgan's waist, chin hooked over his shoulder.

"Missed you," Marshall said against his ear.

Morgan shivered. "You were only gone eight hours."

"Still too long."

They stayed like that until the water cooled, trading slow kisses, hands wandering without urgency. When they stepped out, Marshall wrapped Morgan in a towel, dried him with the same care he'd use on something fragile and priceless. Morgan returned the favor, kneeling to towel Marshall's legs, dropping open-mouthed kisses to the inside of each thigh. Marshall's cock thickened, but Morgan only smiled and stood.

"Bed," Morgan said. "I'm not done with you."

The bedroom was dim, curtains drawn against the city glow. Marshall had left the bedside lamp on low; its amber light painted Morgan's skin in warm tones as he pushed Marshall gently onto the mattress. The sheets were flannel, soft from a hundred washes, smelling of their detergent and the faint cedar of the closet. Morgan crawled up the bed to straddle Marshall's hips, knees bracketing his waist.

Marshall's hands settled on Morgan's thighs, thumbs stroking the crease where leg met groin. Morgan leaned down and kissed him slow, the caress filthy, tongue sliding against Marshall's until they were both breathing hard. When Morgan sat back, his cock curved up against his belly, a bead of precome glistening at the tip.

"Want to feel you," Morgan said. He reached for the nightstand and pulled out the bottle of flavored lube they kept there. "Like at the cabin. Just us."

Marshall nodded, throat tight. Morgan slicked his palm, then wrapped his fingers around both their cocks, holding them together. The first slide was an electric rush of hot, wet, and perfect. Morgan set a lazy rhythm, hips rocking in counterpoint. Marshall moved his hands to Morgan's ass, spreading him slightly, and let his thumbs brush the sensitive skin behind his balls.

"Like that," Morgan whispered. "Don't stop."

They moved together, unhurried. The city murmured beyond the windows, but inside, there was only the slick sound of skin, the creak of the bed, and Morgan's soft moans each time Marshall's cock dragged against his. Marshall watched Morgan's face, his eyes half lidded, lips swollen, a gorgeous flush spreading down his chest. He looked debauched and cherished all at once.

Morgan shifted, releasing their cocks to brace his hands on Marshall's chest. He scooted forward, leaning towards the headboard, knees sliding wider, until his cock bobbed just above Marshall's mouth. Marshall didn't hesitate. He licked a stripe up the underside, swirled his tongue around the head, tasting salt, cherries, and Morgan. Morgan's thighs trembled.

"Marshall, ah God."

Marshall took him in, slow, letting Morgan set the depth. Morgan's hips rolled gently, fucking Marshall's mouth with shallow thrusts. Marshall kneaded his ass, encouraging, one finger tracing the rim of his hole but never breaching, just teasing pressing a promise with each graze of his finger against the nerve-rich pucker.

Morgan's rhythm faltered, a whine building in his throat. "Close," he gasped. "I—Marshall, I want. So much."

Marshall pulled off, lips shiny. "Come here."

He guided Morgan back down, arranging them chest to chest, cocks trapped between sweaty bellies. Morgan's mouth found Marshall's, and he kissed him messy and desperate. They rocked together, the angle perfect now, delicious friction building fast. Marshall slipped a hand between them, wrapping it around both shafts, stroking in time with their hips.

Morgan buried his face in Marshall's neck, teeth grazing the tendon there. "Love how you feel," he mumbled. "Love."

The words dissolved into a moan as he came, pulsing hot between them. Marshall followed seconds later, groaning Morgan's name like a prayer. They stayed locked together, trembling, until the aftershocks faded.

Morgan was the first to move, rolling to the side but keeping one leg hooked over Marshall's hip. He reached for the towel draped over the footboard and wiped them clean with lazy swipes. Marshall watched him, thumb brushing Morgan's lower lip.

"You said love," Marshall murmured.

Morgan's eyes flicked up, suddenly looking embarrassed and shy. "I did."

Marshall pulled him close, kissed his temple. "Good."

They dozed, tangled and warm, the city's heartbeat a lullaby. When Marshall woke later, moonlight had replaced the lamp's glow. Morgan was awake, tracing patterns on Marshall's chest with one finger.

"Can't sleep?" Marshall asked, voice rough.

"Thinking," Morgan said. He propped his chin on Marshall's sternum. "About how this place doesn't feel like yours anymore. Feels like ours."

Marshall's heart stuttered. "Yeah?"

Morgan nodded. "I want to leave something here. Something that's mine." He hesitated. "I brought a plant. It's in the kitchen window. A little succulent. Needs sun."

Marshall smiled into the dark. "We'll give it sun."

Morgan's finger paused over Marshall's heart. "And I want to cook for you. Tomorrow. Something fancy. I looked up a recipe—risotto with mushrooms. I'll burn it, probably, but—"

"I'll eat it anyway," Marshall said. He rolled them so Morgan was beneath him, caged by arms and warmth. "Burned risotto and succulents. Sounds like home."

Morgan's eyes went soft. "You're not scared?"

"Of what?"

"Of me. Staying. Needing." Morgan's voice cracked on the last word.

Marshall kissed him, slow and thorough, until Morgan melted beneath him. "I'm scared of waking up and you not being here," he admitted against Morgan's lips. "That's all."

Morgan's arms came up, wrapping around Marshall's neck. "Then don't wake up alone."

They made love again, slower this time. Morgan on his back, knees drawn to his chest, Marshall between them, frotting with deliberate strokes, mouths fused. When Morgan came, it was with Marshall's name on his tongue and tears overflowing his eyes. Marshall followed, spilling across Morgan's belly, then licked him clean with lazy swipes of his tongue until Morgan was giggling, oversensitive.

After, they showered again, this one quick and playful, Morgan stealing kisses under the spray. Marshall first dried Morgan's hair with the towel, then his own. They padded naked to the kitchen, where Morgan reheated leftovers while Marshall poured wine into mismatched mugs. They ate standing at the counter, hips bumping, feeding each other bites from the same spoon.

Later, back in bed, Morgan curled into Marshall's side, head on his chest. The succulent sat on the windowsill, moved to the bedroom like a tiny green promise. Marshall carded his fingers through Morgan's damp hair.

"Tell me something true," Morgan whispered, echoing their cabin ritual.

Marshall thought for a moment, then rephrased something he'd told Morgan weeks ago. "I used to think love was a debt," he said. "Something you paid back with interest. But this—" he pressed a kiss to Morgan's forehead, "—this is interest I'm happy to pay forever."

Morgan's smile was small, fierce. "I love you," he said, clear and steady. "Not because you saved me. Because you see me."

Marshall's arms tightened. "I love you too. Every sharp edge and soft center."

Outside, the city kept moving, headlights sweeping across the ceiling and a dog barking two floors down. Inside, there was only the hush of breath, the warmth of skin, and the quiet certainty that tomorrow would bring burned risotto and watering cans and two toothbrushes in the same cup.

Morgan fell asleep first, fingers curled loosely around Marshall's wrist. Marshall stayed awake a little longer, listening to the rain start against the window, watching the succulent's silhouette in the moonlight. He thought of the cabin and the joy they'd found there. He thought of the apartment that was no longer just his.

Then he closed his eyes and followed Morgan into dreams.

***

Morgan

"Ellis, wait until you hear what the guys came up with." He slipped into a seat in her office. "We want to propose a charity game to the GM and the owners, with funds going to help LGBTQ+ kids play. Jake is convinced we can fast-track it, have it all lined up in seven days. We can organize the actual event like those in Campbell's program, or the ones at the YMCA that Mr. Davies volunteers at. I'm thinking the day after the game, we do a full reveal, leveraging one of your many plans for helping me come out." He grinned as he sucked in a breath. "This finally feels right."

She stared at him for a moment, then turned to a filing cabinet. She used a key on her keychain to unlock one of the drawers, looking over at him to ensure he'd seen her security, probably on his behalf. Ellis pulled out a folder at least two inches thick and transferred it to her desk. She flipped it open and went through the different dividers he could see were labeled with the alphabet.

"I don't think anything before P would work," she muttered, still shuffling her way through the divided sections. Oh, here's P. I think we can work with this, given everything else—" She looked up at him. "—that you don't know about the other things. How did you find a solution that would dovetail with the league's and Mr. Davies' plans?" She shook her head. "Never mind, doesn't matter. Morgan, I've got a plan for this."

"League plans? And the GM has a plan?"

"Oh, not for you, but the league is pushing diversity hard this year. Most teams have charity things planned, but none have gone so far to do a nonregulation game. I think it's a great idea." She pulled the divider out of the folder, setting the bulk of the paperwork to the side. "Mr. Davies pitched new policies to the league that strengthen the protections queer athletes can depend on. Supports to have in place for out and queer players at every level of hockey. He had a league meeting last week."

"Last week? He was at the hearing last week."

"Yeah, he made sure he flew back in time from headquarters." She grinned. "He's very protective of his players, you know."

"Yeah, he was my coach for a long time."

"Okay." She picked up the papers and circled around the desk. "Let's go find an empty meeting room and get started with planning. I can already tell you that the GM and owners will be very open to something like you guys are proposing. I have enough confidence that I want to iron out details before we get their permission. The sooner it happens, the better for you. Coming out later in the season would be extra hard, since we're defending the Cup. Now is good, as far as I'm concerned."

He followed her down the hallway, his step lighter than it had been in a long time.

***

Two days later Morgan stepped out of the arena into the cool October night, the buzz of the Zamboni fading behind him as the team's laughter lingered in his ears. The parking lot was quiet, the streetlights casting long, jagged shadows across the asphalt. He adjusted his bag on his shoulder, the weight familiar, and headed towards his truck, keys jingling in his hand.

A figure stepped from the shadows near a parked sedan, the flash of a phone camera catching Morgan off guard. "Morgan Oakson?" The voice was sharp, female, with a practiced edge. A woman in her thirties, notepad in hand, her coat buttoned against the chill, approached with a purposeful stride. "Nua Chen, SportsGains. Got a minute?"

Morgan's stomach dropped, his pulse spiking as he scanned her face for intent. Burke's threats echoed. *"You can't hide forever."* And for a split second, he wondered if she knew. "Uh, it's late," he said, voice tight, taking a step towards his truck. "Practice tomorrow. What's this about?"

Nua's smile was professional, but her eyes were sharp, searching. "Heard about the Dingoes' charity game pitch to the league. Sounds like a big deal for the community. A good deal. There's going to be queer inclusion and a youth outreach. You're a key part of it, right?" She tilted her head, pen poised. "Anything personal driving that? Fans are curious about the real Morgan Oakson."

His throat tightened, the air suddenly too thin. The team's plan, their support, felt exposed under her gaze, falling apart like a play called too early. "Just team effort," he managed, forcing a casual shrug. "As an organization, we wanted to do more for marginalized groups. Now, we're all in it for the kids." He gripped his keys harder, the metal biting into his palm a distraction from the panic clawing up his spine.

Nua scribbled something, her eyes never leaving his. "Sure, but you're the star defenseman. People want your story. Any chance you're sitting on something big? Maybe tied to the trial rumors floating around?" Her tone was light, but the question landed like a body check.

Morgan's heart thudded fast, like he'd been at a bag skate, the parking lot shrinking to a tunnel of fear. *She knows something.* "I really need to get going," he said with a smile, voice deliberately calm even though his pulse was racing. He turned towards his truck. "You could probably get a media handout if you talk to Ellis, our PR manager. Have a good evening." He climbed in, slamming the door. His hands shook as he started the engine.

Nua lingered, her silhouette framed in his rearview mirror, jotting notes as he pulled away.

"Speaker, text Ellis."

"What do you want the text to say?"

Well, wasn't that a thousand-dollar question.

"Media outside rink. Nua Chen. I don't remember who she's with. Asked about charity game and then the trial."

The personal assistant in the speaker read the text back to him, and with a final "Send it," he notified Ellis that everything was falling apart.

The drive home was a blur, the highway's white lines morphing with his thoughts.

Burke making good on his threats. The trial that seemed to be moving slow as molasses. And now the media tracking me down. When will it stop?

Ellis's "what-if" scenarios played on a loop in his head, and now here one was, as if she'd spoken it into being, and it was real and breathing down his neck.

He gripped the wheel, resolve hardening. *I won't let him control this.*

The team's charity game, their raised glasses flashed in his mind. He wasn't alone, but the spotlight was closing in, and he'd need to decide how to face it.

***

Morgan

Morgan laced his skates in the locker room, the familiar scent of liniment welcome after the parking garage's sterile chill. Jake's laughter boomed as he recounted a bar story, while Riley attended to his goalie gear with quiet focus. For his part, Thompson was draped over the edge of the bench, tossing a puck up and catching it. The team's rhythm was a defense, their chatter a reminder of the family Morgan had fought to keep.

Everything old is new again.

These details had happened before every practice skate and game. Each player had their own routine, and it seldom varied from game to game. Hockey players were notoriously superstitious, something Morgan could testify to.

"Thompson, do you have all your teeth?"

Surprised at the question, he stopped tossing the puck up and nodded. "All my chompers are accounted for."

"Might want to find a less aggressive toy to play catch with, especially right over your face."

"You ruined it, Oakkie. I can't do my tosses anymore if I'm going to be worried about taking a puck to the face."

"You do what you want, Tommy, but my money's on Morgan's statement coming true. Once you start thinking about that kind of failure, it's nearly always a sure bet to happen." Riley shook his head. "Now that he said something, your bloody face is all I can see when I look at that puck." He shivered. "Give it to the equipment guy. Get him to dunk it in holy water or something. Now," he glared at Morgan, "I've got to begin again. You messed me up."

Morgan mimed zipping his mouth shut, but his grin broke through.

God, I love these guys.

On the ice, Morgan fell into the first drill, his blades carving sharp arcs as he snapped a pass to Thompson, their chemistry as tight as ever. The puck hit the tape with a satisfying *thud*, and Thompson grinned, returning a quick return pass that Morgan deflected with ease.

"Still got it, Oakson!" Thompson called, skating backward, his stick raised in mock salute.

Morgan's chest warmed. The rink was a refuge where Burke's threats felt distant, the courtroom's weight lessening with each stride.

But as the drill wound down, Morgan's eyes flicked to the stands. A figure stood near the glass, unfamiliar yet unsettling, their silhouette sharp against the empty seats. Not Burke—this person was too short, too slight— but something about their posture, the way they watched, sent a chill down Morgan's spine.

He glanced at Jake, who'd noticed, too, his grin fading as he skated closer.

"You know that guy?" Jake asked, voice low, his stick resting on the ice.

Morgan shook his head, his pulse quickening. "No, but it feels off." He scanned the stands again, but the figure was gone, melted into the shadows like the parking lot scare. Coach Masterson's whistle cut through the chatter, calling the team to take a knee on center ice, but Morgan's focus was stuck on the empty seats, Burke's whisper, *"You'll regret this"*, echoing faintly through his mind.

After practice, Jake lingered by Morgan's side as they headed to the locker room. "Could be a scout. Could be nothing," Jake said, slapping at Morgan's shoulder. "But we're watching, yeah? Nobody messes with our guy." His tone was light, but his eyes were serious. The vow steadied Morgan's nerves.

As they stripped off gear, Thompson piped up, tossing a towel at Morgan. "Yo, charity game's got buzz already. Heard some fans on social media talking about Pride tape, rainbow jerseys. You're starting something big, man."

The team's nods, their easy support, sparked a fire in Morgan, a defiance against the stranger's shadow. But as he left, glancing at the stands one last time, the unease clung, a reminder that Burke's reach, or the media's, might not stay confined to courtrooms.

***

Morgan

As the team clomped their way into the locker room, ready to shed their practice gear and skates, Morgan caught a glimpse of Coach Matheson following them. He shoved at Jake's shoulder and nodded towards the door. "Wonder what he wants?"

"Not sure," Jake said, gaze fixed on their coach. "He looks pleased, whatever it is."

"Listen up," Coach called loudly. "Cop a squat somewhere, boys."

Morgan didn't need to be told twice. He was already in front of his locker so he just turned and sat on the bench, Jake beside him.

Thompson was across the room, and he looked to be mouthing words at Morgan, but his overemphasis on whatever it was made it indecipherable.

"Thompson, wanna share with the class?" Coach must have noted the same thing Morgan had.

"No, sir," Thompson said, shaking his head. "Nothing at all, sir."

"Tracy, pass out the ballots and pencils."

Tracy was Coach's assistant, and the younger man made the rounds, handing every player a small piece of paper and a short pencil.

"It's time to pick a new captain. Gonna miss Greer, but this is a chance for someone else to step up and be a game maker from the locker room to the rink. Now, what you're going to want to do is write down the name you want to nominate for captain. If I agree with you, it'll be a done deal, but I'm reserving veto rights."

Thompson's hand went up, and Morgan saw Coach's jaw clench and flex a few times before he gritted out, "Thompson, what?"

"We shouldn't nominate ourselves, should we?"

"If you nominate yourself, I'll definitely be using my veto power."

Laughter rose around the room in a wave, lessening the tension in the air.

Morgan didn't have to think about his selection for more than a second before writing down Jake's name and folding the paper in half. Tracy ran the rounds in reverse, picking up each folded ballot. He then stepped to the side and ran through the nominations before handing Coach one piece of paper. Coach looked down, and a tiny smile curled the corner of his mouth.

"Guess I don't have to veto anything. Tracy, how many votes did he get out of all of them?"

"Twenty-one out of twenty-two."

"Boys, say hello to your new captain." He reached in his jacket pocket and pulled out a bright new "C" that would be applied to the captain's jersey. "Jake, come get your letter."

Morgan watched as a thousand shifting emotions flooded across Jake's face before settling finally into a sheepish pride. Jake stood and clomped to where Coach stood, accepting the bold letter that would tell every opposing player as well as the officiating personnel that Jake had the trust of his team and was authorized to speak on their behalf.

Thompson cupped his hands around his mouth, shouting, "Speech, speech." The cheer was picked up by every player until the room rocked with the demand of their new captain.

"I don't know what to say," Jake said, looking down at the letter in his hand. "I'm honored and humbled by your trust. My goal will be to rev everyone up at every game and to push the refs to target the other team with every penalty." Laughter rippled around the room. "No, seriously, guys. Thank you."

"Okay, playtime's over. Everyone needs to get changed and hit the weight room unless you're scheduled for a trainer." Coach slapped Jake's shoulder. "Well earned, Jake. You'll do great."

As soon as Coach Matheson and Tracy had left the room, the volume level rose markedly, each player offering their own congratulations. When Jake came back and sat next to Morgan, he still looked slightly shellshocked.

"You're made for this, Cap." Morgan laughed. "Been cutting your teeth on Thompson and Riley all this time. Didn't even know you were in training, did you?"

"I didn't expect this."

"Which is exactly why you're the right person." Riley spoke up from across the room. "Hey, I'm curious—who'd you put for your pick for captain?"

"I didn't write my name down, if that's what you're asking."

Morgan shook his head. "No, just wondering who you saw as your competition." He shrugged, "Right, Riley?"

"Yeah, who'd you nominate?" Thompson was already out of his sweaty gear and into the shirt and shorts they'd all wear to the gym. "Was it me, Jake? It's okay to say it was me."

"You're such a suckup, Thompson." Jake finished pulling off his pads. "Let's get going, boys. Unless you want a bag skate tomorrow?"

"Already going to your head?" Morgan asked with a grin.

"I'll only use my power for good, promise."

CHAPTER FOUR

Morgan

Morgan sat on the familiar couch in Dr. Sanchez's office, a mug of calming tea slowly growing cold on the side table. The sheer normalcy of it all was small comfort against the storm in his chest. *Take my wins where I can find them.* The clock ticked softly, sunlight filtering through sheer curtains, casting moving patterns on the carpet.

The courtroom's tension still gripped him, Burke's whispered threat mingling with older wounds, like the ones left by his father's voice, cold and cutting, calling him weak for showing emotion, dismissing anything less than a "real man's" toughness.

With everything else going on, he found the thought of following Ellis's plans paralyzing. He was consumed with the fear of losing hockey. He knew that outcome wasn't really something he had to fear as long as he kept performing on the ice, but it still felt like the only lifeline he could still control. As if once his sexuality were exposed, the fans would gnaw at the bones of his career, a shadow that felt too real after Burke's glare. On the other end of the equation was his growing relationship with Marshall. He hadn't been home in days, living out of a duffel bag tucked underneath his side of Marshall's bed.

Morgan found himself grinning. He loved the idea of having a side.

Dr. Sanchez leaned forward, her calm eyes steady. "What's driving this fear, Morgan? Losing hockey. Where does that connect?"

He rubbed his hands together, knuckles whitening. "It's like…I mean, if I'm outed, the fans, the league, they'll turn. I just know they will. Season ticket fans will cancel, and the team has to follow the money, you know? Hockey remains a stronghold of toxic masculinity and misogyny. Slurs like queer and gay are still thrown around in the locker room by a few of my own team. On the ice it's usual to be called a…Well, I don't want to say what they call anyone not in their own jersey. My team's better than most, but that could be the impact of having a queer GM. Right now, hockey's all I've got. Maybe all I'll ever have. My dad made it clear anything other than being a successful professional player was failure. My mom's been silent for months. Now, it feels as if by being gay, I'm betraying hockey, risking everything I've fought for." His voice cracked, but he pushed on. "Burke's threats make it worse, like he's still got me on a leash."

"You're not on anyone's leash," Dr. Sanchez said, voice firm but kind. "Your father's disapproval shaped you, but it doesn't define you. You're a hockey player and a gay man. Those identities can coexist. *Do exist.* Integrating them, owning both, that's your power. You've already started by telling many on your team and your mom. Build on that."

Morgan exhaled, the words sinking in, an echo of the breakthrough he'd had when he first trusted his teammates. The fear didn't vanish, but it felt less like he was in a cage. He nodded. "I want that. To be whole, not split."

The session ended, and he left, lighter, and ready to face the ice with both parts of himself, Burke's shadow a little smaller.

***

After a reasonably quick drive, Morgan stood on his mother's porch, the suburban street quiet except for the rustle of autumn leaves skittering across the pavement. It was hard to believe he'd grown up here. The house, a modest two-story with sections of peeling paint, felt smaller than he remembered, its familiarity diluted with distance. He hadn't talked to her since last season, since her hesitant "I'll try, honey" over the phone, her love tangled with worry.

His knock was soft, almost reluctant, the weight of the courtroom still heavy in his chest.

The door opened, and his mom stood there, still as pretty as she'd always been. "Morgan," she said. Her voice was tentative, as if she wasn't sure it was him.

He swept her up in a hug, holding her close. "Hi, Mom."

"Come inside, Morgan. I'm glad you stopped by." She held the door for him, then closed it after he'd made his way through. "Go to the kitchen. I'll make us some coffee."

He followed the familiar path to the kitchen, then leaned against the center island as he watched her slowly work on a pot of coffee.

"How have you been, Mom?"

"Oh, I'm okay. Go ahead and sit at the table, honey. This won't take a minute to brew."

It wasn't long before she brought the pot to the table, giving it to him to pour them each a mugful.

"I read about the court case in the news," she said, sitting across from him, the hand holding her coffee shaking visibly. "The trial coverage. I didn't know how bad it was with that man." Her voice cracked, guilt flickering in her eyes. "I should've called. I just...I didn't know how. I'm so ashamed of myself, Morgan. I should have been there for you."

Morgan's throat tightened, the old wounds from his father's disapproval mixing with her hesitation. "I didn't make it easy," he muttered, rubbing suddenly sweaty palms on his jeans. "I shut you out after I told you. About me. About being gay. I was scared you'd be done...?" He trailed off to silence, the words too heavy to bring out into the light.

She leaned forward, reaching for his hand, then stopping short. "I was wrong to pull back. I was scared too. Of losing you, of not understanding. But I see you now, Morgan. You're so strong, stronger than your dad ever knew." Her voice steadied, eyes glistening. "I'm proud. I think I just need time to catch up. To get used to the idea."

Morgan exhaled, the knot in his chest loosening. "I'm trying to be open, Mom. With the team, maybe the world. There's this charity game we're planning for queer kids. I want to do it right, but I'm scared of losing everything." His voice dropped, the fear raw. "Including you."

She reached for his hand again, this time holding tight, her grip firm despite the tremble. "You won't lose me. I'm here, learning. Just keep me in the loop, okay?" She smiled, tentative but warm, and Morgan felt a spark of hope, like a puck finding the net after a long fight.

As he left, he ran their conversation back through his head, finding hope in every word. The courtroom's weight, Burke's threats, it all felt lighter, his mom's love a connection to a part of himself he'd thought lost.

***

Marshall

The equipment room smelled of sweat and winning and the ghost of the last practice.

Marshall had the door half shut behind him, one shoe still in the hallway, when Morgan slipped in after him like a shadow. The rink was quiet. It was the lunch break, various crews scattered to their trucks or food court, most players headed home for their noontime nap.

Morgan had on his compression layer, the gray shirt clinging to his chest like a second skin. A streak of red cut across one cheekbone, an abrasion from an errant stick, and his hair was messy with sweat. He looked filthy and edible. Marshall's mouth went dry.

"Lock it," Morgan said, voice low, already reaching. "Nobodys' going to notice the GM and one defenseman missing for a handful of minutes"

"There's no lock on this side." Marshall pulled the door closed, and the click echoed like a gunshot in the narrow space. Shelves of pucks and skate guards rattled as Morgan pushed him back against the wall. Their mouths crashed together. There was no hello, no softness, just teeth and tongue and the scrape of Morgan's teeth against Marshall's jaw. Morgan tasted like coffee and the oranges he'd shared with the team an hour ago.

"Been hard since you bent over the boards," Morgan muttered against Marshall's lips. His hands were already at Marshall's belt, yanking leather through the metal buckle. "Fuck, look at you."

Marshall groaned, hips jerking forward. His own hands went to Morgan's ass, hauling him closer, grinding their clothed cocks together. The friction was maddening, at once too much and not enough. Morgan's breath whooshed out as he dropped to his knees on the gritty floor without ceremony.

"Off," he ordered, tugging Marshall's slacks down just far enough to free his cock. It sprang out, thick and flushed, a bead of precome already pearling at the slit. Morgan licked it away with a flat swipe of tongue, then took Marshall to the root in one slick slide.

Marshall's head thunked back against the wall. "Jesus God."

Morgan pulled off with a wet pop, grinning up at him, lips shiny. "Quiet, old man. Don't need the whole team knowing we're getting a little afternoon delight."

He dove back in, cheeks hollowing, his hand twisting at the base in time with his mouth. Marshall's fingers tangled in Morgan's hair, not guiding, just holding on. The world rocked faintly with every bob of Morgan's head. Outside, someone laughed and a radio crackled as life went on past the steel, three feet away.

With his free hand, Morgan shoved his own clothing layer lower, palming his cock through his boxers. The outline was obscene, his dick long, curved, straining. He pulled off Marshall again, spit stringing between them, and stood.

"Want you against me," he panted. "Now."

Marshall spun him, pressing Morgan chest-first to the shelving. A box of pucks clattered to the floor. Morgan's laugh was breathless and the slightest bit wicked. Marshall yanked the leggings down to Morgan's thighs, boxers following. Morgan's cock jutted out, flushed dark, slick at the tip. Marshall freed his own again, slotting behind him, sliding his length into the cradle of Morgan's ass.

"Fuck, yes," Morgan hissed. He braced one forearm on the shelf, reaching back with the other to grip Marshall's hip, urging him closer. Marshall spat into his palm, slicked Morgan's cock, then wrapped his big hand around it, gripping tight and stroking fast. The angle was perfect, giving him access to acres of scalding hot skin, the drag of veins silken beneath his palm.

They moved fast, hips rolling, the shelves creaking in protest. Morgan's forehead dropped to his arm, muffling the moans that kept trying to escape. Marshall leaned over him, chest to back, beard scraping the nape of Morgan's neck.

"Gonna come all over your pretty ass," he growled.

"Do it," Morgan gasped. "Mark me up, make me feel you all fucking day—"

Marshall's rhythm stuttered. He bit down on Morgan's shoulder through his shirt to muffle his groan as he came, pulsing hot between Morgan's cheeks. The feeling of his come painting Morgan's skin must have sent Morgan over. He shoved back hard, cock jerking in Marshall's fist, adding to the mess in thick ropes that dripped onto the floor.

They stayed locked like that, panting, trembling. Marshall's forehead rested between Morgan's shoulder blades.

After a beat, Morgan laughed the sound shaky, but entirely delighted. "Think we just baptized the equipment room."

Marshall huffed a laugh, pressing a kiss to the bite mark blooming under cotton.

Morgan twisted, kissing him sloppy and quick. "Cleanup on aisle three."

"Worth it."

They used several of the team towels to wipe down. Morgan tucked himself away, straightening up, looking only slightly less debauched. Marshall did the same, then cupped Morgan's face, thumb glancing gently across the red mark on his cheek.

"Clock's ticking," he said.

Morgan stole one more kiss, nipping Marshall's lower lip. "Tonight. Your couch. I'm riding your thigh 'til I can't walk."

Marshall's cock gave a valiant twitch. "Get back to work, trouble."

Morgan unlocked the door and slipped out onto the arena's lower concourse like nothing had happened. Marshall counted to ten, adjusted himself, and followed.

He knew the equipment room would still smell like sex when the manager next went in.

CHAPTER FIVE

Morgan

The Dingoes' executive meeting room, a large space tucked off the main corridor on the third floor, security doors protecting the C-wing, buzzed with purpose. Inside the room, its whiteboards were scrawled with play diagrams and marker streaks.

Coffee mugs, some chipped and one emblazoned with *Dingoes Bite*, cluttered the table, steam curling in the fluorescent light. Morgan sat between Jake and Riley, the warmth of their presence easing the knot in his chest. The queer-friendly charity game, first proposed over beers, was almost ready to launch, its roots in Morgan's partial coming-out to the team now a spark for something bigger.

Ellis had been here for most of the conversation and greenlighted every idea they'd had. It felt good to know the team, or hell, the whole organization, had his back.

Jake leaned forward, his broad frame dwarfing his chair, and gestured at a whiteboard timeline. "All right, we can book ice for the charity game next week. We're adding on a youth skills clinic, fan meet-and-greet, and funds for LGBTQ+ inclusion programs. Morgan, you got ideas for outreach?"

Morgan's fingers tapped the table, nerves flickering but steadied by the team's trust. "Yeah," he said, voice firm. "I was thinking we partner with local queer youth groups, get them on the ice with us. Show them hockey's for everyone." He paused, then pushed deeper, the weight of his truth lighter here. "I hid who I was for years, scared it'd end my career. Burke, well, you know how he used that against me, made me feel small. I want kids to know they don't have to hide."

Riley's eyes softened, his normally fidgeting hands still as he nodded. "That's powerful, man. Let's make it happen. Those summer clinics are a good opportunity too. Maybe we can do a scholarship."

Across the table, Thompson grinned, jotting notes. "You're speaking from the gut, Oakson. Fans'll feel it."

The room hummed with calls confirming sponsorships, league approval of their jersey designs for the charity game, and plans for a post-game online auction of game-worn gear. Each idea knit the team tighter. Morgan felt the bond solidify, a far cry from the isolation of his past with Burke.

As they wrapped up, Jake clapped his shoulder. "Dingoes protect Dingoes, yeah?"

Morgan nodded, the team's unity proving to be a shield, and he added his voice as part of their fight.

***

Morgan

Morgan stood in Ellis's office, the faint hum of the building's cooling system seeping through the walls, a familiar anchor amidst the chaos of his thoughts. The desk was cluttered with drafts of press releases and a cool-looking mock-up of a rainbow-striped jersey, the charity game's logo bold across the chest. Marshall leaned against the wall, his eyes steady on Morgan, a quiet promise of support.

Ellis tapped her tablet, pulling up a revised version of Plan P. "We're set for the announcement after the charity game," she said, her voice brisk but warm. "You'll do a press conference, short and direct, framing your story around inclusion and the youth clinics. We've got the league's backing, and Marshall's new policies will amplify the message." She glanced at him, her smile tight but encouraging. "You ready to own this, Morgan?"

Morgan's pulse quickened, the remembered threat of being forcibly outed pressing against his ribs. The courtroom's tension even before Burke's whispered threat mingled with the media's potential for disaster in his mind. But Jake's words, *"Dingoes protect Dingoes,"* echoed, giving him something to hold onto.

"Yeah," he said, voice steadying. "This is my decision. I want to do it for me first, but also the kids and for the team. But, and I know I've asked this a dozen times, what if the fans turn?"

Marshall stepped forward, his presence filling the small space, his voice low and measured. "Real talk. Some fans might. And there's going to be shitposting on social media. We can't stop that from happening, and the owners are aware." He shrugged and smiled. "But the league's shifting, Morgan. My policies to set up reporting channels and wellness programs are all in place to protect you and others who have stayed closeted for longer than they want. And the team's all in." His eyes locked with Morgan's, a spark of warmth beneath the professional restraint. "At this point in history, you're not just a player. You're leading something bigger."

Ellis nodded, flipping to a new slide, a mock-up of a social media campaign with #DingoesForAll, lining out plans to feature Morgan and the team at the youth clinic. "We'll flood social media with positive posts, drown out the noise. But I got a call from Nua Chen this morning. She's got a source claiming 'personal turmoil' tied to the trial. Nothing specific, but she's pushing for an exclusive before we go public."

Morgan's stomach dropped, the memory of Nua's sharp gaze in the parking lot flashing like a warning. "She's not getting it," he said, jaw tight. "This is my story. Our plan." He glanced at Marshall, their shared look a silent vow, the slow-burn heat of their connection simmering beneath the surface.

"Good," Ellis said, tapping her tablet. "We'll lock down the press conference details tomorrow. We have a good script, we know the timing, and now I've got to get on the media invites. Marshall, can you coordinate with the league for extra security? Just in case Burke's circle gets wind and tries anything."

Marshall nodded, his hand brushing Morgan's arm as he moved to grab his phone, the touch fleeting but electric. "On it. We've got your back, Morgan." The words carried weight, a promise beyond the rink, and Morgan felt a spark of courage, the charity game and his truth no longer a burden but a chance to reclaim his narrative.

As they finalized details, Morgan pictured the kids at the clinic, their faces bright with possibility, and the team's raised glasses at the bar. The fear of being outed still lingered, but with Ellis's plan and Marshall's steady presence, it felt like a fight he could win.

CHAPTER SIX

The season opener was an away game, and from the beginning of the game, the Narwhals' arena started at a low growl. The crowd's murmurs rose to a roar of hostility even as the puck dropped, its sharp clack echoing off the boards.

Morgan skated hard, the ice spraying under his blades, the scoreboard glaring 2-1 against the Dingoes in the third period.

His shots kept going wide, which was frustrating. He'd watched a wrist shot sail over the crossbar, then a one-timer that at least rang the gong, clipping the left post, and each miss tightened the vise in his chest. The game's slump mirrored a game from months ago, when pressure had cracked his focus, and now Burke's courtroom glare haunted him, whispering failure.

He chased a loose puck, his legs heavy, his mind clouded. A Narwhals defender bodychecked him into the boards, the glass rattling, crowd jeering. Morgan gritted his teeth, pushing back, but his next pass to Thompson was sloppy, picked off by the Narwhals' offensive center. The buzzer sounded, the score now 3-1, and Morgan turned to skate to the bench, head low.

Jake clapped him on the shoulder, his brand-new "C" shining bright on his shoulder, then their newly minted captain was over the boards to play the puck drop with the first line. It wasn't long before Morgan's teammates stood at the boards, waiting. He vaulted the wall, skates firm on the ice as he chased a Narwhals forward down the ice. He couldn't catch up, but thankfully Thompson, ever steady, covered for him, blocking the breakaway with a diving poke-check. On their way back to the bench, Thomas muttered, "Got you, man," fist-bumping Morgan's glove.

In the locker room after the loss, Morgan overheard media interviews out in the hallway, the questions of a couple of the reporters turning to him, talking about how "Oakson's distracted, off his game."

The words stung like salt in a wound. Burke's threat to leak his secret loomed, and the pressure of defending their Cup win from last year made every miss feel like it was done in even more of a spotlight. But Thompson's save and his quiet nod helped. The ice was still his, slump or not, and he'd fight to keep it.

***

Morgan

The YMCA gym buzzed with the nervous energy of a well-attended hockey clinic, even with holding it early in the morning. The Dingoes had a game tonight, and the timing had been the stickiest part to schedule. There were at least a dozen queer youth in borrowed hockey gear stumbling across a makeshift rink, their sticks clattering against pucks. Morgan stood at the edge, his Dingoes hoodie loose over his frame, watching Jake demonstrate a wrist shot, his booming laugh drawing grins from the kids.

Off to the side, Riley crouched by a shy teen, helping adjust their grip, while Thompson, ever the show-off, spun a puck on his stick, earning cheers.

Morgan's chest tightened as memories of his own teenage years, interminable days of hiding who he was, the ice his only escape, came flooding back. These kids, with their rainbow wristbands and tentative smiles, were why the charity game tomorrow mattered. He stepped onto the shiny surface, the slick synthetic ice tiles making his sneakers slip slightly, and knelt beside a kid who was maybe fifteen, with a buzzcut and nervous eyes, clutching a stick too big for them.

"First time on the ice?" Morgan asked, his voice soft, mirroring Marshall's tone.

The kid nodded, their shoulders tense.

"I was scared, too, my first time. Thought I'd fall flat. But you've got this." He tapped the kid's stick, guiding their hands. "Keep it low, snap your wrist. Like this."

The kid tried, the puck skidding but connecting, their face lighting up. "Holy crap, I did it!" they said, voice cracking with excitement.

Morgan grinned, the kid's joy a mirror to his own when he'd found hockey, a refuge from his father's disapproval.

Jake skated over, lobbing a puck Morgan's way. "You're a natural, Oakson. These kids are eating it up." He lowered his voice, eyes serious. "You're giving them something we didn't have. Keep going, man."

"Thanks, Captain." He grinned at Jake, who rolled his eyes.

As the clinic wound down, the kids gathered for a group photo, their sticks raised, Morgan in the center with Jake and Riley flanking him.

A teen with a Pride pin on their jacket tugged Morgan's sleeve. "You're, like, a big deal, right? Thanks for this. It means a lot." Their voice was shy, but their eyes held a spark Morgan recognized, of hope, defiance, and the start of something new.

Morgan nodded, his throat tight. "Means a lot to me too."

As the kids left, he lingered, the gym's warmth a contrast to the Narwhals game's cold sting. The charity game wasn't just a plan—it was a promise to kids like these, and to himself, that they could be whole. Burke's shadow felt smaller here, the team's support and the kids' courage a fire that burned brighter than his fear.

***

Morgan

Morgan slumped on the locker room bench, the air thick with the stench of sweat and tape adhesive, the clatter of gear being tossed into bags a sharp counterpoint to his racing thoughts. Their second 3-1 loss to the Narwhals stung even worse, his missed shots replaying like a taunt, amplified by the media's murmurs about his "distraction."

With so much happening, seemingly all at once, the fear of being outed before he was ready twisted his gut. But Jake and Riley flanked him, their presence a wall against the noise.

Jake tossed a water bottle his way, its cold plastic slapping against Morgan's palm. "Screw the reporters," he said, voice gruff but warm. "You're in a slump, not a soap opera. We've got your back, Oakson."

Riley nodded, stripping off to his compression layer, wet with sweat. "Yeah, man. Media's fishing for drama. You're still our guy. It's too early in the season for them to jump on someone like they are. Assholes."

Their loyalty, solid as the team's pact from months ago, steadied him, a reminder of when he first shared his truth.

Morgan exhaled, leaning forward, elbows on knees. "Thanks, guys. It's just everything. I'm scared I'll be outed before Ellis's press release is sent out. If we don't control the messaging, it has the potential to tank everything. Hockey, the team." His voice wavered, but saying it aloud felt like shedding weight.

Jake's jaw tightened. "Let them try. None of them, no reporter and surely not that joke of an ex, *none* of them have any power here. Dingoes protect Dingoes."

The words wrapped around Morgan like armor, his fear of Burke's potential leak shrinking under their support. He stood, feeling safer, the locker room's chaos now a haven. The slump was temporary; his team was not.

***

Morgan

Morgan sat on his apartment couch, here for the first time in a couple of weeks. It felt more like a hotel room than a place that was his, the room's dim lamplight glancing across the bare walls.

Home's with Marshall.

His phone buzzed, an unknown number flashing, and his gut twisted, the ever-present fear of being outed surging like a phantom pain.

He answered, voice cautious. "Hello?"

"Mr. Oakson, this is Daniel Tolly, representing Burke Hammond." The voice was smooth, practiced, a lawyer's tone that set Morgan's nerves on edge. "My client wishes to settle this matter privately. He's prepared to drop any public statements if you withdraw the restraining order violation charges."

Morgan's head swam, forcing him to take in a full breath, his free hand clenching into a fist. "Public statements?" he said, voice tight. "You mean his threats to out me? To ruin my career?" The words spilled out, raw and defiant, the fear of the news leak mingling with Burke's old control.

Tolly's tone stayed even. "My client believes a mutual agreement benefits both parties. Consider it, Mr. Oakson. You have until the next hearing to decide."

The call ended, and Morgan's phone slipped from his hand, landing on the couch with a soft thud. He couldn't catch his breath, the apartment suddenly feeling too small, Burke's shadow creeping back like damp fog. He grabbed his phone and dialed Marshall, the ringing a lifeline in the dark.

"Morgan?" Marshall's voice was sleepy but alert, a balm against the panic. "What's wrong?"

"Burke's lawyer," Morgan said, words tumbling out. "They're trying to pressure me to drop the charges. Said he'll keep quiet if I do. It's...it's like he's still got me cornered." His voice cracked, but he pushed on. "I can't let him win, but I'm scared, Marshall. The press conference, the game. We're so close."

Marshall's tone hardened, protective. "He's bluffing, Morgan. He's desperate because you're strong. You've got the team, Ellis, and me. And we're not going to let him control this or anything else." There was a pause, then softer, he said, "You're safe. I'm here. Want me to come over? Or do you want to come my way?"

Morgan exhaled, the offer tempting, but tomorrow's announcement held him back. "No, I'm okay. Just missed you." He pictured Marshall's steady gaze, the rink's chill on his skin, the team's raised glasses. "I'm doing the press conference. My way."

"That's my guy," Marshall said, pride clear in his voice. "Get some rest. We've got this."

The call ended, and Morgan leaned back. The apartment felt less oppressive, Marshall's words and the team's support a shelter against Burke's threat. The press conference loomed, but so did the charity game, a chance to turn fear into something good.

***

Morgan

Morgan's phone buzzed as he pulled into the parking lot, the morning air crisp and sharp. A text from Ellis, marked urgent.

Meet me in my office. Now.

His stomach dropped, the memory of the reporter's probing questions in the bar parking lot flashing like a warning light. He jogged to the management wing, the familiar hum drowned out by the thud of his pulse.

Ellis's office was a whirlwind of papers and coffee cups, her tablet glowing with a news article. She looked up, her expression a mix of frustration and determination. "SportsGains sent over a piece an hour ago," she said, turning the tablet towards him. Just like in his nightmares, the headline on the document screamed, "Dingo Star's Secret: Trial Hints at Hidden Personal Life."

Morgan's breath caught, the words blurring as he scanned the article. It was vague but damning, mentioning the restraining order, Burke's name, and "unconfirmed rumors" about Morgan's involvement.

"It's not explicit," Ellis said, her voice steady despite the tension. "But it's close. Nua Chen's been digging, and someone, maybe court staff, maybe Burke's circle, leaked enough to get this out. I've responded to them with the hopes they'll kill it, but we need a plan. Fast."

Morgan sank into a chair, gripping the armrests, Burke's courtroom whisper, *"You'll regret this,"* ringing in his ears. "They're gonna out me," he said, voice low, the fear he'd voiced to Dr. Sanchez now real. "Before I'm ready. Before the charity game today."

Ellis leaned forward, her eyes fierce. "Not if we get ahead of it. Plan P's ready. We have your announcement, tied to the charity game, framed as your story. We can release it now, and it's so well done, it won't look like it was just reactive. You control the narrative, Morgan, not Nua Chen or Hammond." She slid a draft press release across the desk, the words "Dingo Defenseman Morgan Oakson Proudly Supports Diversity in the Sport" bold and clear.

Morgan's chest tightened, the weight of the decision crushing. He thought of the team's fist bumps, his mom's tentative smile, and Marshall's steady gaze. "What if it backfires?" he asked, voice raw. "The fans, the slurs..."

Ellis's expression softened. "Some fans might turn. But your team won't. The league's behind you. And now Marshall's policies are gaining traction. And those kids at the charity game? They need you to show them it's possible. The clinic received only positive reporting that I saw, and the blowback on social media wasn't what you might have expected. It wasn't all roses and champagne, but it wasn't bad." She tapped the release. "Your call, but we're running out of time."

Before he could respond, Jake burst in, his face flushed from practice. "Heard about the article. Screw SportsGains. Ellis, we want to put out a team statement that Dingoes stand with Morgan, man. Rainbow jerseys, Pride tape, the works." He grinned, fierce and unyielding. "Let's make it loud."

Morgan exhaled, the team's loyalty a relief. "Ellis, do you think your kill-it demand will actually get a result?"

"Honestly?" She made a see-saw motion with one hand. "Maybe, maybe not. I worded it very strongly. I should know within the hour."

"Okay." He nodded at Ellis, resolve hardening. "Regardless of what they say, let's not react. I want to do the release as we originally planned. Plan P. P for Pride. My way."

The fear didn't vanish, but it shrank, dwarfed by the fire in Jake's eyes and the promise of the charity game.

CHAPTER SEVEN

Morgan

The Dingoes' locker room buzzed with post-practice energy, the air thick with the scent of sweat and liniment, the clatter of gear bags a familiar rhythm. Morgan sat on a bench, tightening the laces on his sneakers, the massive changes just around the corner weighing heavy on his shoulders. The social media posts asking, *What's Oakson Hiding?*, still swirled in his mind, but the team's presence, their easy chatter, made it easier to breathe.

Jake plopped down beside him, his broad frame taking up half the bench, a towel slung over his shoulder. "Yo, Oakson, you ready to shut down the social noise?" he asked, his grin infectious as he offered a roll of rainbow tape. "You're gonna kill it."

Riley, peeling off his goalie pads, nodded from across the room. "Yeah, man. We're all in, we've got those rainbow jerseys, the works. Those kids that were at the clinic? They're gonna lose it when they see you out there doing your thing." His voice was quiet but firm, his eyes steady.

Thompson, leaning against a locker, chimed in, his lanky frame slouched but his smirk sharp. "Heard some fans on social forums are already hyped for the game. The hashtag DingoesForAll is trending, thanks to you. Screw the haters." He tossed a puck Morgan's way, the black rubber skidding across the bench. "Tape that stick and show 'em who you are."

Morgan caught the puck and traced its rough edges, a smile tugging at his lips. The team's warmth, their unyielding loyalty, was protection against the media storm, against Burke's venom. He accepted the offered roll of tape from Jake.

"Thanks, guys," he said, voice steadying. "Didn't think I'd get here, but you're making it real."

He cleared the old tape with a practiced series of twists and tears and then wrapped the Pride tape around his stick, the colors vibrant, a promise to the kids at the charity game and to himself.

As the team filed out, Jake clapped Morgan's shoulder, his grip firm. "Dingoes protect Dingoes, yeah? We'll be in the stands tomorrow, cheering you on."

The locker room's chaos faded, but its warmth lingered, Morgan's resolve hardening like ice under pressure. The press conference was still to be conquered, but with his team behind him, he felt ready to step into the light.

***

Morgan

Morgan sat in the local league office, the polished mahogany desk gleaming under fluorescent lights, its barren shine a stark contrast to the familiar chill. Beyond floor-to-ceiling windows, the city skyline sprawled, a maze of glass and steel that felt worlds away from the ice. Gary sat beside him, his agent's steady presence a counterpoint to the nervous energy thrumming through Morgan's veins. He was still tired from practice but felt like he could skate a dozen shifts. Across the desk, two men in crisp suits and a woman with a kind but sharp gaze listened, their notepads open, pens poised. The weight of Burke's media tip, the media posts swirling with hints of his "secret," had pushed Morgan here to disclose his truth privately before it was stolen.

He took a breath, his hands clasped under the table to hide their tremor. "I'm gay," he said, voice clear despite the tightness in his throat. "My ex, Burke Hammond, was abusive. He violated my restraining order multiple times and has repeatedly threatened me. Extortion. That's what the rumors that are circling are all about. The court case is against him and the chaos he brought. I'm telling you because I want to play hockey, not hide. But I'm not ready for the world to know yet. Not until the press conference. Ellis has worked out a very good plan, and I have confidence in her, the owners, and in the team." The words hung in the air, raw and heavy, a leap he'd feared since his father's voice first called him weak for showing emotion. "Also, I don't want to do the conference before the game. I don't want to make this game today about me. It's about all the kids *like* me, giving them a chance to see themselves laced up and on the ice." He cleared his throat. "That's all I wanted to say."

The woman, Director of Player Welfare, leaned forward, her pen pausing, eyes warm but professional. "Morgan, thank you for trusting us. The league stands with you, and your privacy and safety are our top priorities. We'll coordinate with your PR team to protect you, whether you stay private or go public." She glanced at her colleagues, who nodded.

One of them, a grizzled VP with a championship ring glinting on his finger, added, "You're a Dingo, a champion. This doesn't change that. We've got your back, like your GM's new policies ensure."

Gary squeezed Morgan's shoulder, his grin subtle but proud. "Told you, kiddo. You're covered."

Relief flooded Morgan, a warm tide against the fear that had haunted him for so long. The league's support was a pleasant surprise, the bridge between his identities of hockey player and gay man seemingly easier to cross than he'd imagined possible. He thought of the charity game, the kids at the YMCA, their rainbow wristbands and tentative smiles, and felt a spark of purpose.

"Thank you," he said, standing to shake hands, his grip steadier. "I want to do this right, for the kids, for the game."

As they left, Gary clapped his back, their steps echoing across the hallway's polished floor. "You're stronger than you know, Morgan."

The office's calm lingered in Morgan's chest, the weight of secrecy lifted, if only in that room. He pictured the rink, the team's fist bumps, Marshall's steady gaze, and felt lighter, ready to face whatever came at him on the ice with both parts of himself, Burke's shadow growing ever smaller.

***

Morgan

Morgan sat in Dr. Sanchez's office, the familiar leather chair creaking under his weight, the scent of lavender and old books a calm counterpoint to the storm that would soon be raging on social media. Sunlight filtered through sheer curtains, casting patterns on the carpet, the trees movement with the wind a quiet rhythm that steadied his racing heart. Ellis's Plan-P script was waiting in his email, but the furor on the rumor sites still clawed at him, a ghost of his father's voice calling him weak.

Dr. Sanchez leaned forward, her calm eyes piercing but kind. "You told the league this morning," she said. "That was a big step, Morgan. How does it feel holding both parts of yourself, integrating as a hockey player and a gay man?"

Morgan rubbed his hands together, knuckles whitening. "It was freeing, like I said to Marshall. But scary too. Social everywhere is blowing up with rumors, and I'm afraid the fans will turn, that in spite of everyone's reassurances that it'll all be okay, I'll still lose hockey. It feels like it's all I've got, you know? I know in my heart that's not true." He thumped a fist against his chest. "But the game, this charity game, it's become so important to me. That game is for kids like I was. Kids who are hiding or scared. I want to be for them what I didn't have."

She nodded, jotting a note. "You're combining those parts, Morgan. That's your strength. You know, owning your truth, not just for you but for others. The press conference is a chance to reclaim that narrative we've talked about. What's one thing you want to hold onto as you step into it?"

Morgan exhaled, picturing the YMCA kids, Jake's Pride tape, Marshall's steady gaze. "The team," he said, voice firmer. "They're my anchor. And the kids? They need to see it's possible to be out and still play." The words felt like a vow, the fear of Burke's shadow shrinking under the weight of his purpose.

"Good," Dr. Sanchez said, her smile warm. "Hold that close. You're not alone in this, Morgan. You've built a community."

The session ended, and he left. The office's calm lingered, a bridge to the press conference, where he'd face the world not as Burke's victim but as a man whole in his truth.

*****

Marshall

Marshall leaned against the boards, the ice quiet under dim lights as he waited for Morgan after the team's morning scrum. The arena was a safe zone, its silence a stark contrast to the media storm brewing on social media, where posts about Morgan's "secret" multiplied like cracks in the ice. Ellis's text about the league meeting glowed on his phone, pride swelling in Marshall's chest for Morgan's courage, but worry gnawed beneath it, a familiar ache. Burke's treachery could spiral out of control, and the whispers on social media were already loud, threatening the cautious bonds he and Morgan had built.

As General Manager of a team that held to the goal of inclusivity, Marshall was pushing for anti-harassment policies at the league level, inspired by Morgan's fight and his own sister's quiet battle against abuse years ago, and maybe even because he'd felt he had no choice but to stay closeted through his entire playing career.

This was personal, his and Morgan's connection a tightrope he walked daily, balancing duty with the warmth that flared every time Morgan was near. He clutched his clipboard, its edges worn from countless practices, and pictured Morgan in the league office, baring his truth, a flame of courage Marshall vowed to protect.

Morgan appeared from the tunnel, eyes tired but warm, a flicker of relief in their depths. "League took it well," he said, stepping close, his voice low to keep it private. "It was bizarrely easier than I thought, saying 'I'm gay' to strangers. Weird, but really freeing. Knowing you and the team are in my corner is huge. I can't say thank you enough." His hand brushed Marshall's, a fleeting spark like their most recent stolen kiss mere hours ago, charged but restrained, the rink's chill amplifying the heat.

Marshall's heart ached, the urge to pull Morgan closer warring with their agreement to stay professional in public. He nodded, his voice steady despite the pull. "You're doing more than you know, Morgan. The league, the team, me—we're all here, on your terms." He paused, his gaze softening. "The charity game, your story. All of it is combining to change things for those next players. The next gen, if you will. I'm proud." The words carried weight, a vow beyond where they were now, and Morgan's small smile, tentative but real, lit a spark in Marshall's chest.

The silence wrapped around them, their growing love a quiet strength amidst the storm. Morgan's fingers lingered near his, but Marshall stepped back, honoring their restraint.

"I wanna go home," Morgan said, his voice soft. "You coming, Marshall?" He turned, his silhouette sharp against the ice.

"I won't be long." Marshall watched Morgan disappear into the tunnel, the dim lights casting long shadows across the ice, the air thick with frost and the faint echo of skates from earlier practice.

His clipboard felt heavy, but tonight it was Morgan's courage that weighed on him, a fierceness that both inspired and challenged his restraint.

Ellis's text about the plans buzzed on his phone.

Morgan's ready. Plan P's a go.

Marshall exhaled, picturing Morgan on the ice, his passes crisp despite the slump, his eyes warm despite the storm. The charity game loomed, a chance to amplify Morgan's truth, to show kids like those at the YMCA that hockey could be theirs too. Marshall's heart ached, pride and worry intertwined, their bond a promise worth guarding through all the battles ahead. He turned from the rink, the ice's silence upholding his vow to stand by Morgan, no matter the cost.

***

Morgan

Morgan sat in his truck outside, the engine idling, the night air cool through the slightly opened window. His phone glowed with social media posts, the hashtag DingoesForAll trending alongside the loathsome "Dingoes Star's Secret" headline. The media storm had split the internet. Some posts were cruel, speculating about his "personal drama," while others were unexpectedly supportive.

A fan account with a rainbow avatar posted that *Oakson's a champ, whatever his story. #DingoesForAll*. A youth hockey group chimed in: *Can't wait for the charity game! Morgan's fighting for us.* This kind of support, raw and real, caught Morgan off guard, a warmth cutting through the hate.

But the vitriol stung, those slurs and sneers from anonymous accounts echoes of his father's voice. *"You're not man enough."*

One post, liked hundreds of times, read *Oakson's hiding something. No place for that in hockey.* His chest tightened, the fear surging, but the supportive posts from fans, kids, even a retired player, all combined to light a spark. He thought of the YMCA clinic, the kid with the Pride pin, and remembered their shy "Thanks for this."

He texted Ellis.

Seeing some good stuff on social. Fans stepping up. Let's make the press conference big.

Her reply was instant. *Hell yeah. Script's tight, we're ready.*

Morgan exhaled, the truck's rumble steadying him. The hate was loud, but the support was louder, a chorus of allies he hadn't expected. He pictured the charity game, rainbow jerseys flashing under rink lights, and his resolve hardened. Burke's shadow, though shrinking, still loomed, but Morgan wasn't alone. He had a whole village between the team, fans, kids, and Marshall, all ready to stand with him. He put the truck into Drive and went home to Marshall's apartment.

CHAPTER EIGHT

Morgan

Morgan stepped out of his apartment building into the cool October night, the streetlights casting a dim yellow glow across the suburban parking lot, their flicker painting jagged shadows on the asphalt. The air was sharp, tinged with the scent of wet grass from an earlier rain, and his breath fogged as he fumbled with his keys, the metal cold against his palm.

His truck was only a few steps away, a familiar refuge, but a shadow shifted near the edge of the lot, and the acrid sting of cedar and musk hit him like a bodycheck. The scent dragged him back to that same old tired apartment. Back to Burke's voice hissing, *"You're nothing without me,"* and the pain of that final, desperate escape flooding his senses. His heart slammed against his chest, every nerve screaming to run, but his feet froze in place, rooted by months of Dr. Sanchez's lessons.

You are not that man anymore.

Burke emerged, his compact frame looming under a flickering streetlight, eyes cold and predatory, glinting like blades in the dark. "Morgan," he growled, stepping closer, his voice low but toxic, dripping with the control he'd once wielded. "You think a restraining order is going to stop me? A little piece of pathetic paper? Cute. I want fifty grand, or I'm telling the world your dirty little secret.

Every fan, every player, every reporter. We'll see how long you last after I get through with you." His smirk twisted like a knife in Morgan's gut, the threat echoing the internet posts that had haunted his phone for hours.

Morgan's knees trembled, and he squeezed his fist, the keys biting into his palm. In the next moment, though, he planted his feet, drawing courage from the team's raised glasses, Jake's fist bumps, and Marshall's steady, loving gaze. "You're done, Burke," he said, voice steady despite the fear clawing up his spine. "The police know. The league knows. I'm not yours to control anymore." The words echoed Dr. Sanchez's *"Reclaim your narrative"* mantra and the memory of the upcoming charity game's rainbow everything, the kids' cheers at the YMCA clinic—all of it fueled his defiance.

Burke's laugh, sharp and cruel, sent a shiver through him, but Morgan held his ground, hand on his phone, the preprogrammed SOS text to Gary and Ellis glowing ready. Burke took another step, the night's silence amplifying the crunch of his boots, the threat a living thing in the air.

Morgan backed towards his truck, his pulse a drumbeat, but his eyes never left Burke's. He thought of all the things in the works, all the plans, everything coming together to give him the chance to own his truth, to stand with his team for kids like he'd been. That little boy who'd been scared, hiding, but dreaming of the ice.

"You don't scare me anymore," he said, voice low, a lie that felt truer for the saying.

Burke's smirk faltered, his eyes narrowing, but Morgan's thumb hovered over the SOS, and he finally tapped it, ready to admit he needed help. Ready to call in the cavalry that had his back.

***

Marshall

Marshall's car screeched into the apartment lot, tires skidding on damp asphalt, his pulse racing as Gary's urgent text burned in his mind.

Burke's at Morgan's place RIGHT NOW, violating the order again!

The night was dark, with haze thick under flickering streetlights, their yellow glow barely cutting through the damp air. His eyes locked on Morgan, backed against his truck, his frame tense but defiant, and Hammond, who stood way too close, his predatory stance a threat Marshall felt in his bones.

Thank the gods I live close by.

The scent of wet grass and exhaust mingled with the adrenaline, and riding above all of that was his discipline from his decades first as a player, then a coach, all of that experience honing his calm despite the rage simmering beneath.

He stepped out of the vehicle, his voice steady but commanding as it cut through the night's silence. "Hammond, back off. You're done here." His tone carried the weight of authority, but his heart clenched at Morgan's wide eyes, the fear there tempered by trust as their gazes met.

Hammond spun, sneering, his compact frame coiled like a snake, but Marshall gained ground, positioning himself between them, a shield rooted in duty and something much deeper. He was already dialing 911, fingers steady despite the urge to do more, to erase the threat Hammond posed to Morgan's hard-won peace.

"911, what is your emergency?" The operator's voice came through sharp and clear.

"A man is being menaced by someone he has a restraining order against. 72910 Withal Drive, just inside the parking lot," Marshall said, his eyes flicking to Morgan, whose shoulders were easing slightly, a spark of relief in his gaze.

"Is anyone injured?"

"Not yet," Marshall said, his voice firm. "This is Marshall Davies. I'm a friend of Morgan Oakson. The man threatening him is Burke Hammond, currently under bail restrictions."

"I've got officers headed your way now. Stay on the phone, Mr. Davies."

"I will." He kept his eyes on Hammond, whose bravado faltered, a slow step back betraying uncertainty as sirens wailed in the distance, their red and blue flashes cutting through the haze as they pulled into the driveway to the apartments in record time.

"Marshall—" Morgan's voice was tentative, a soft tether, and Marshall nodded.

"I know."

Officers swarmed, their boots loud on the asphalt, cuffs clicking as they pinned Burke, his threats dissolving into curses. "Morgan Oakson, restraining order violation," an officer confirmed, hauling Hammond to a cruiser, his silhouette shrinking under the flashing lights.

Marshall met Morgan's gaze, willing him to understand he was now and would always be safe. The slow-burn heat of their bond pulled beneath the professional restraint. Glaring red and blue lights strobed the entire area, and as the sirens faded, Marshall exhaled, relief mixing with worry, his thoughts turning to the promise to protect Morgan through the battles ahead.

He gave a statement and then lingered for the police interview of Morgan. Afterwards, he steered Morgan to his car. Seeing him climb in the passenger seat, make himself comfortable, and buckle up was something Marshall wanted so badly in his daily life, he could have wept. Instead he walked around the hood and dropped into the driver's seat. He reached over to flip on the seat warmers, the night's chill a reminder of the fragility they guarded, their connection a quiet strength.

***

Morgan

The Dingoes' locker room hummed with energy, the air thick with the scent of sweat and tape adhesive, the clatter of gear hitting the floor in a familiar rhythm. Morgan sat on a bench, lacing his sneakers, the weight of the confrontation with Burke still heavy in his chest.

Jake plopped down beside him, his broad frame taking up space, towel slung over his shoulder. "Heard about what happened, man," he said, voice low but fierce, his eyes searching Morgan's. "Hammond pulling that crap in your parking lot? Screw that guy. You okay?" He clapped Morgan's shoulder, the gesture heavy with a deep loyalty.

Thompson, leaning against a locker, bulked-up arms folded across his chest leaving him looking every bit the devastating defenseman he was. "You're tougher than he'll ever be, Oakson. All the team stuff we've got going on, and you're still here leading this thing, man. But you're not alone. We've got your back. I'll defend you any day." His grin was sharp, but his eyes held a warmth that steadied Morgan's nerves. He tossed a roll of Pride tape Morgan's way, the rainbow colors catching the light.

Morgan caught the tape. As he traced its vibrant colors, a smile tugged at his lips. "Thanks, guys," he said, voice steadying. "Last night was rough, but you, Marshall, the police—you're why I'm still standing. I'm ready for the press conference, to do this for the kids." He thought of the YMCA youth, their rainbow wristbands, and the charity game's promise of a chance to show them hockey was theirs too.

Jake stood, fist raised for a bump. "Dingoes protect Dingoes, yeah? We'll be there, front row, when you tell the world."

The team's nods, their easy loyalty, wrapped around Morgan like a shield. As they filed out, the locker room's chaos faded, but its warmth lingered, Morgan's resolve hardening like ice under pressure, ready to face the press conference with his team behind him.

***

Morgan

Morgan sat in Dr. Sanchez's office, the familiar leather chair creaking under his weight, her ever-present pot of soothing tea steaming on the side table. The lamp's warm glow softened the room's edges, casting patterns on the carpet, but Burke's ambush lingered in his mind, that damned cedar-and-musk scent a ghost that till haunted Morgan. The clock's soft ticking was a stable rhythm, soothing in its simplicity.

"I stood up to him," Morgan said, voice low but firm, his hands clasped to hide their tremor. "Last night, in the parking lot. Burke came at me, demanded money, threatened to out me. I was terrified. I thought for sure that he was going to hurt me again, like before, when I couldn't fight back, when his fists left bruises I hid from the team. I think knowing I had already escaped helped steady me." The memory of hiding, broken and scared in that first desperate attempt, contrasted sharply with the defiance he'd summoned, fueled by every experience of living out from under Burke's daily physical threats.

Dr. Sanchez leaned forward, her calm eyes piercing but kind. "You faced him, Morgan. That's not just surviving, that's thriving. The fear's real, and you've got the scars to prove that reality, but standing up in spite of it, while drawing on your strength—that's the definition of courage. What did it feel like, saying those words to him?"

Morgan exhaled. "Telling him off was powerful. Like I wasn't the guy who ran anymore. It's crazy because I could have spit words back at him then, but I didn't. And now that part of me still waiting for the next hit is less present. Still there, like he's not really gone, but I'm less fearful." He thought of the terror he'd felt and shivered. "Marshall came for me. That's what kept me standing. The guys have been so good about it too. Lots of threats of bodily harm to Burke."

Dr. Sanchez smiled gently, jotting a note. "You've built a community, Morgan. That's your power now, learning to lean on them, letting them lift you. The press conference, the charity game, all the plans you've put into play—they are extensions of that strength. What's one thing you want to carry into those moments?"

Morgan pictured the rink, the team's Pride stickers, Marshall's hand brushing his. "Hope," he said, voice steadier. "Yeah, hope. For me, and for the kids who need to see pro hockey's possible, even if you're queer."

The session ended, and he left, the lingering calm of the office like a warm jersey.

Later, in his apartment, Morgan needed a connection to Marshall. It was his volunteer night at the YMCA, so he wasn't surprised when Marshall didn't pick up. Morgan's voice was soft but sure in the voicemail. "Thanks for last night. I'm okay because of you. You matter to me, Marshall. I wanted you to know."

A reply came hours later, a text.

YMCA night, sorry. Always here. Rest easy.

The words warmed him, their cautious relationship a quiet strength, fragile but still growing. Morgan sank into bed, the night's silence no longer a threat. Unlike during those sleepless nights haunted by Burke's fists, he drifted off soundly, the weight of Burke's shadow lessened, the charity game and press conference a beacon of a brighter future.

CHAPTER NINE

Morgan

Morgan sat in Ellis's office, the space a blend of professional order and team pride, the faint hum of the cooling system seeping through the walls. Her laptop glowed on a sleek desk, its case plastered with Dingoes logos, a chipped mug reading "Dingo Pride" holding pens beside a stack of media binders.

Morning light slanted through blinds, catching dust motes as Morgan shifted in his chair, nerves buzzing like a serious case of pregame adrenaline, the weight of Burke's parking-lot ambush and the social media storm tightening his throat. Ellis and Gary sat to either side of him, their presence and confidence echoing the strategizing that took place months ago when Morgan first considered going public.

Ellis tapped her laptop, pulling up a draft statement honed over the past few days, its words bold and clear: *Morgan Oakson, Dingo defenseman, proud gay man, abuse survivor, champion.* "We keep it authentic, Morgan," she said, voice crisp but warm, her eyes meeting his with quiet encouragement. "You share your truth. That you're gay, proud, and a Dingo through and through. We'll frame it around your strength, your championship grit, the charity game's mission. Backlash *is* possible—of course it is. But we've got counterstrategies with vetted interviews, team support highlights, and getting #DingoesForAll trending." She nodded to Gary, who leaned forward, his tie slightly askew, his grin a reminder of the trade that had given Morgan a fresh start.

"League's behind you, kiddo," Gary said, his voice steady. "I know I've said it before, but your contract's ironclad, and the Dingoes are all in. We'll have security inside and outside the meeting room, just in case, and I've got a service lined up for you for a few weeks, post-announcement." He paused, his eyes softening. "I recommend telling the whole team tonight, before the sports news world explodes. They deserve to hear it from you."

Morgan exhaled, fingers drumming the armrest. "I hate thinking that I'm going to have to come out to each years' roster. I already did it once last year, why can't that be enough." He sighed again. "I'm just complaining. I know I should. I will. Tonight. I'm scared. Of losing fans, dealing with slurs, or even still losing hockey, but I'm done hiding. I want to do it right, for the kids at the charity game, for me."

He scanned the statement. His story laid bare was a truth he'd once thought would end him. Now, here he was, ready to pull the trigger on releasing everything. The office's background noise and the distant clatter of rink maintenance was familiar and soothing. He thought of Marshall holding his hand and felt a spark of courage.

He nodded, resolve as solid as a perfect pass hitting the tape. "We're still scheduled for after the charity game. If they're up for it, I'd love the team with me there. I'll know tonight." He stood, shaking Ellis's hand, his grip firm. "Thanks for putting up with my waffling. This isn't easy." Turning to Gary, he grinned, clapping his shoulder, shaking him playfully in his chair. "My rock. You always do right by me, Gary."

Gary laughed, his eyes crinkling. "You make me money, kiddo. But I'd do it for free. You're one of the good ones." His face softened, a rare vulnerability, and Morgan felt the certainty of their friendship beyond the client relationship, part of the bridge to the future he was building.

***

Morgan

Morgan stood at center ice, the Dingoes' logo beneath his skates, the chill biting through his practice jersey as the team gathered around him. The lights gleamed in sparkles off the ice, the stands empty but the air heavy with anticipation, the clatter of sticks and gear bags fading as his teammates waited. Jake leaned on his stick, his broad frame relaxed but attentive. The circle of faces were Morgan's friends, his teammates, his tribe. They were loyal, unwavering, and supported Morgan without question.

At least right now they do.

He took a breath, his pulse racing. "Guys," he said, voice low but clear, "I'm telling you first because you're my family. I'm gay. Been hiding it for years, scared that coming out would end my career. My ex is the one behind the rumors. He keeps threatening to out me, and I want to come out on my own terms. I'm done hiding. I'm coming out at the press conference after the charity game. For the kids, but mostly for me."

The rink fell silent, the weight of his words settling like fresh ice.

Then Jake stepped forward. "You're our guy, Oakson. Gay, straight, whatever. Doesn't matter because you're a Dingo. We've got you." His grin was fierce, a vow formed in loyalty.

From the corner of his eye, Morgan spotted movement, but before he could recognize who the player leaving was, Riley was in his face, nodding and speaking, his voice quiet but firm. "Those kids at the charity game? They'll see you and know they belong. That's huge, man." He gripped Morgan's shoulder for a moment, his touch steady, a promise of protection.

Thompson threatened Morgan with a thrown puck, because of course he did, then smirked, eyes sharp but warm. "That conference is gonna be lit. Hashtag DingoesForAll, right? Screw the haters."

The team erupted in nods, gloves raised, the circle tightening around Morgan, their warmth protection against the fear of backlash.

Morgan exhaled, a smile breaking through. "Thanks," he said, voice steadying. "I want you guys there, if you're up for it. Means everything." He thought of the charity game, the rainbow flags, the kids' cheers, and felt his resolve harden. The press conference was no longer a threat but a chance to lead.

As the team skated off, Jake lingered, a firm fist bump coming in again. "Dingoes protect Dingoes," he said, and Morgan nodded, the rink's chill a promise of strength.

***

Marshall

Marshall stood at the large opening of the team's box, the ice below looking like a gleaming sheet of clear glass under bright lights, the air crisp with frost and the faint echoes of skates. The players clustered around Morgan at center ice, near the Dingoes logo, their gloves raised for fist bumps, a circle of loyalty that warmed Marshall's chest. He noted one player—third-line forward, number 17, nearing retirement—skate to the gate, his absence a shadow on the moment. The player's planned exit after this season softened the sting, but Marshall's thoughts stayed with Morgan, his courage shining brightly as he shared his truth with the team.

"I'm thinking that went well," Ellis said from behind, her heels clicking as she entered the box, her tablet glowing with all their plans.

Marshall turned, his expression neutral despite the warmth in his chest. "I agree. How'd he do with you about the press conference?" Morgan's wave caught his eye, a brief spark that Marshall returned with a nod, their bond a quiet pulse.

"Really well," Ellis said, her voice brisk but warm. "We finalized Plan P. Finally. It's authentically Morgan, through and through, and tied to the charity game. Gary's worried about security, so he's hiring a service for Morgan, twenty-four/seven for a couple weeks. That's the only new piece." She paused, her eyes sharp but kind. "There's something we haven't covered in our releases."

Marshall's brow furrowed, his grip tightening on the railing. "What do you mean?"

Ellis stepped closer, her voice low. "I'm not blind, Marshall. I've seen the way you and Morgan look at each other when you think no one's watching. You've kept it professional, but if the sports press catches even a whiff, they'll make everyone's lives miserable. It's just not done." Her tone was firm, a warning wrapped in support. "The timing of his arrival followed by yours? They'd have a heyday, and you'd be the one dragged through the mud."

"I have nothing to confess, Ellis," Marshall said, his voice steady, the memory of Morgan's hand brushing his in the dim light flickering in his mind. His role as GM demanded restraint, but his feelings were a truth he guarded.

"If there ever is, make me your first call," Ellis said, her smile softening the edge. "We protect our own."

"I will," Marshall said, turning back, the Zamboni's slow sweep leaving smooth ice in its wake, a mirror for his resolve. "We will." He pictured Morgan at the press conference, and vowed to shelter him as best he could, their bond a promise worth guarding, even if it meant navigating the tightrope of professionalism alone.

CHAPTER TEN

Morgan

The atmosphere inside the Dingoes' rink came alive with energy for the queer-friendly charity game. The stands were packed with fans waving rainbow flags, their cheers a vibrant roar that echoed off the rafters, drowning out the memory of Burke's threats. They had pulled players in from a wide array of divisions and leagues, spreading the chance to support inclusive play far and wide. Ellis had told him yesterday that every team approached had sent at least one player.

Pride stickers gleamed on all helmets, a bold nod to the LGBTQ+ inclusion cause sparked by Morgan's courage, their shine catching the bright rink lights. The ice sparkled, the scent of freshly groomed ice sharp in the air mingling with the buzz of community support. There were several different youth groups in matching jerseys and a bevy of locals chanting, "Dingoes Unite!" from the front rows, their voices a chorus of hope.

Morgan skated with purpose, his stick feeling like a natural extension of his body, the weight of the upcoming media storm and the ambush fading under the crowd's warmth. A banner caught his eye, emblazoned with the hashtag DingoesForAll painted in rainbow colors. It was held by a group of teens he recognized from the YMCA, their faces bright with pride. The memory of his own teenage years fueled each of his strides.

Late in the second period, a winger up from the minors fed him a pass, a clean tape-to-tape that Morgan caught mid-stride, the stick's weight familiar in his grip. He deked past a defender, the puck's sharp *clack* against his stick echoing, and ripped a snapshot that clanged the top bar, bouncing down the goalie's back and into the net.

The arena erupted, rainbow flags waving wildly, fans on their feet, their roar a wave that lifted Morgan higher. He pumped his fist, waving to Jake and Riley in the crowd. His slapdash team mobbed him with helmet taps, their laughter loud over the crowd. Thompson, playing on a different line this time, grinned from the bench and shouted, "That's our guy!" Their chemistry, shaped through months of trust building, shone brighter than the scoreboard's 2-0 lead.

Post-game, the players mingled with fans on the ice, and Morgan signed a kid's Pride-themed jersey. The bright sound of laughter and mechanical camera clicks mingled in the air.

A queer youth group leader, her rainbow pin glinting, gripped his hand. "You're showing kids they belong, Mr. Oakson. Thank you."

Her eyes shone, and Morgan's throat tightened, the team's unity a defense against the fear of backlash. He thought of his truth ready to be shared and felt a spark of defiance, as if the rink was a stage for something bigger.

"It's Morgan, and it's my pleasure. That's what I want, for kids to know no dream is out of reach."

She grinned and shook his hand again.

As the crowd thinned, Morgan lingered by the bench, the quiet settling like fresh snow. Marshall approached from the tunnel, his presence a steadying force.

"That was incredible," he said, voice warm, eyes soft with pride.

Morgan grinned, patting the bench beside him. "Couldn't have done it without the team or you." They sat close, their thighs brushing, the contact electric in the dim light. Morgan shared, "Seeing those kids? It hits different. Makes going ahead with the presser feel right."

Marshall's hand found his, their fingers intertwining, and Morgan leaned in. "I'm ready because of you," Morgan whispered, pulling back, pressing Marshall's thigh with his hand, teasing higher before restraint kicked in.

Marshall nodded, his thumb stroking Morgan's hand, eyes dark with want but tempered. "And at the media conference, I'll be there, supporting from the sidelines."

The promise hung between them, a step towards openness, before they parted, the ice gleaming with possibility, Morgan's heart full of the community he'd helped build.

***

Morgan

Morgan once again stood on his mother's porch, the suburban street quiet, the air soft from an earlier rain. The house with its peeling paint and familiar door once again felt smaller than he remembered, a relic of childhood games and his father's disapproval. His knock was soft, hesitant, hampered by the memory of her scant acceptance after his coming-out.

Since he'd been here last, they'd kept in better contact, sharing text messages every week or so. Right now he was riding the high from the charity game's success, the team's cheers, and Marshall's hand in his. It had all conspired to push him here with a need to bridge the gap before the press conference tomorrow.

The door opened, and his mom stood there, her graying hair loose, her eyes widening with surprise, then softening. "Morgan," she said, stepping aside, her voice trembling but warm. The living room smelled of coffee and old books, the same old knitted blanket draped over the back of the couch. She gestured to a chair, her hands fidgeting, mirroring his own.

"I saw the charity game on TV," she said, sitting across from him. "Those kids, the rainbow flags. I saw all those little faces. Honey, I didn't know how much it meant."

Morgan's throat tightened, the weight of her previous disapproval mingling with the hope of her words. "I was scared to tell you," he said, voice low. "About being gay, and definitely about Burke. Was sure I'd lose you, like I thought I'd lose hockey." He paused. "But the team, the game tonight? We're doing it all for kids hiding like I was. I'm going public tomorrow, at a press conference. I needed you to know."

Her eyes glistened, and she reached for his hand, her grip firm despite the tremble. "I was wrong to pull back," she said, voice cracking. "I was scared, didn't understand. But seeing you out there, leading the charge like you are? I'm so proud, Morgan." She squeezed his hand, a connection he'd thought lost forever. "I understand tomorrow is important to you, but I don't think I'm comfortable going. I hope you understand. I'd love to have you over for dinner or something soon. I know I'm not perfect, not by a long shot, but I want to be involved in your life again. You're my son, Morgan, and I miss you."

Morgan exhaled, a smile breaking through, the charity game's cheers echoing in his mind. "I wouldn't ask you to come, but you even thinking about it is amazing. That's enough, Mom. Just keep trying." He thought of the press conference, his truth ready to be shared, and felt a spark of hope. Her support could be a new thread in the network he'd built. "As far as dinner is concerned, would you be okay if I invited Marshall to come?"

"Is that your boyfriend?" The smile had fled her features, leaving them slightly disapproving. "I guess you could ask him, if it matters to you."

"As I see it, he and I are a package deal." Morgan held his breath, waiting for her to deny his statement.

"Then invite him, please."

Her response surprised him, and he leaned over to brush a kiss against her cheek.

As he left, the weight of her silence lifted, the rink and his team waiting to carry him forward.

***

Morgan

Morgan jogged through a suburban park, the early evening air cool against his skin, the crunch of gravel under his sneakers a steady rhythm against his racing thoughts. The sunset painted the sky in streaks of orange and pink, oak trees casting long shadows , their leaves rustling softly in the breeze, a quiet contrast to work's vibrant chaos. His breath fogged in the chill air.

He reflected on his journey over the past months. From escaping Burke's fists, heart pounding in that desperate flight, to finding strength in Dr. Sanchez's office, her calm voice guiding him to *reclaim his narrative*. The team's embrace at the charity game, their pride in one another and raised gloves, had solidified his place among them, a found family that drowned out his father's old voice. His mother's support felt fragile, but he held onto it even as he remembered each of the kids' cheers, Jake's fist bumps, and Marshall's proud smiles. Morgan was no longer the scared kid hiding his truth but a man ready to face the public, to own his story as a gay hockey player.

Pausing by a bench, his breath steadying, Morgan pulled out his phone and called Marshall. "Hey," he said, voice soft but sure, the park's quiet amplifying his resolve. "Today felt so good. The game, the team, the money raised for LGBTQ+ kids. I'm glad you're going to be at the conference. I was wondering if, after, maybe we could get coffee?" He laughed, realizing he'd barely let Marshall speak.

Marshall's low chuckle warmed him, their growing relationship a steady anchor. "Hello to you too. I'll be there, Morgan. Proud of you. Coffee sounds good. In public too. Right on track with our slow and steady, right?" The words echoed their commitment to balance love and hockey, a future they were building step by step.

"Yeah. Steady," Morgan said, dipping his head as he grinned, the sunset's last beams warming his face. He hung up.

As he turned to jog home, is steps were lighter as the park's quiet wrapped around him like a promise. He wasn't careless, not fearless, but resolute. The press conference had become a chance to lead, to show kids just like he'd been that hockey was theirs too. The public awaited, but so did his truth, a future he was shaping with every stride.

CHAPTER ELEVEN

Morgan

Morgan stood at the podium in the Dingoes' media room, the air filled with the sharp clicks of camera shutters. Flashing lights danced across his vision, the room packed with reporters, their notebooks and recorders poised like weapons.

The team logo loomed on the wall behind him, a navy-and-gold anchor, and Ellis stood at his side, her nod a silent encouragement. His heart pounded, his palms damp, but his voice was firm, constructed by months of work rebuilding his strength. He'd moved well beyond being the man who'd been controlled by Burke, or browbeaten by his father. This was his moment to own his truth, no longer dictated by fear.

"I'm Morgan Oakson, Dingoes D-man, and Cup champion," he began, eyes scanning the crowd. "I'm also gay." As planned, he dropped it into the speech as if it wasn't of the utmost importance. He kept talking and watched the emotions flashing across each reporter's face. "I've lived in fear of losing hockey, of being defined by my past, which includes an abusive ex who has tried very hard to control me through blackmail. But I'm done hiding. I'm proud of who I am, and I'm here to play, to win, with my team. That's it. That's the whole truth." The words spilled out, steady and clear, each one a release of the weight he'd carried for so long.

Ellis stepped forward, "Questions?"

The hands went up, so fast Morgan grinned.

As they'd planned, she picked the bigger outlets first, knowing they'd have a broader base of readers and viewers to cater to.

Supportive questions came first. There was a reporter asking about his inspiration for the charity game, another praising his courage.

But then a sharp voice cut through with a blistering tone. "Won't this distract the team? Some fans are going to say it's a publicity stunt."

Morgan's jaw tightened, but he leaned into the mic, his resolve unshaken. "My team's with me. Hockey's my focus as it always has been. I'm here to play, not to please everyone. My goal is always to send the opposing team away disappointed because I'm a Dingo, and I'm here to win. I'm aware that there will be extra scrutiny just because of this announcement, but my goal is that players like me, at every level of hockey, will see what is possible."

The room buzzed with questions, cameras flashing faster, but Morgan stood tall, his truth a shield, ready for whatever came next.

***

Morgan

Morgan sat in his apartment, the dim lamp casting a soft glow over his hockey memorabilia. Social media posts scrolled endlessly on his phone screen, a mix of support and venom sparked by his announcement.

Proud of you, Oakson! #DingoesUnite read one, retweeted by thousands, warming his chest. But others found problems with his truth.

He's just chasing clout. Should stick to hockey.

His throat tightened, the fear of losing his place in the game flaring back to life, but the supportive posts of fans waving rainbow flags, his teammates reposts—they all bolstered him. He wasn't alone. Not anymore. His team and friends stood firm against the chaos.

***

Marshall

Marshall paced his office, the city skyline dark beyond the window, his phone buzzing with league calls. News of Morgan's announcement had spread fast, and while some team ownership praised his courage, others grumbled about "distractions."

Marshall deflected with calm precision, his voice steady. "Morgan's a champion, on and off the ice. His truth strengthens the team and the league." His mind flicked to his sister's fight for freedom, her resilience mirrored in Morgan's stand. Pride swelled, but worry lingered, and he knew any backlash could hit hard.

He texted Morgan. *You're killing it. We've got this.*

The reply, a simple *Thanks*, tightened their promise, a quiet unity amidst the storm.

***

Morgan

Morgan read Marshall's text, a smile tugging at his lips. The social media posts still swirled, some worded with the intention to be cruel, but the support like Jake retweeting a fan's rainbow emoji and a grinning Riley's post touting the adage that *Dingoes stand together* worked to drown out the noise.

He set the phone down, feeling the team's strength wrap around him, his fear of rejection shrinking under their collective embrace.

***

The Dingoes' locker room thrummed with post-practice energy, the air thick with the pungent odor of twenty-four grown men who'd just worked out for four hours, including two hours on the ice. Sticks clattered as players stacked them near the door for the equipment manager. Morgan sat on a bench, his pads already off, still reeling from everything going on.

Jake stood at the room's center, holding up a roll of rainbow Pride tape. "Next game, we're wrapping our sticks again," he declared, grinning. "For Morgan. For the cause. Who's in?"

Riley raised his glove, voice firm. "Hell yeah, Captain."

Thompson nodded, already wrapping his stick, the tape's colors vibrant against the black carbon fiber. "Let's make it loud, Oakson," he said, tossing Morgan a roll.

The team erupted in agreement, players grabbing tape, their chatter a warm shield against the outside world's noise.

It didn't take a genius to read the body language of the only player not actively taping their stick. Morgan walked over to where Gibson was and sat next to him. "I understand that not everyone wants to be involved."

"No, that's not it. My wife's pastor watched the press conference. He's got her convinced that I'm going to wind up a deviant. No offense intended." Gibson scrubbed at his face. "If I show up on the ice with Pride tape on my stick, I don't know what would happen at home."

"Oh, man. I had no idea. No offense taken." Morgan paused for a moment, then continued, "I called my mom back after we won the Cup. Told her I was gay and was going to come out of the closet at some point." He shook his head. "The first thing she offered was a suggestion that I might want to talk to her pastor. That was nearly the last straw. For a long time, I wasn't willing to talk to her at all. It's been a slow road rebuilding our relationship after that. Religion is a hard nut to crack. Let me know if you figure that one out."

Gibson stared at him. "Your own mother wasn't supportive? You didn't take the Cup home for your day?"

"Nope. It's something I've tried to come to peace with. Like I said, we're working on rebuilding, but nearly every contact is my doing. Some days, I think she'd be happy never talking to me again."

"Let *me* know if you figure that one out." Gibson raised a hand. "Hit me, Jake." A moment later a fresh roll of Pride tape landed in his hand.

"You don't have to do that." Morgan's throat tightened. "We're good."

"Be better when the whole team's decked out. You're slackin', Oakson."

"Okay. Okay." Morgan joined in, wrapping his stick, the tacky pull of the tape a familiar ritual. "Thanks, guys," he said, voice thick. "Didn't know how much I needed this." The idea of his teammates' loyalty being so strong, they were making the locker room a haven made him feel accepted, his truth no longer a burden but a badge.

As the team dispersed, Morgan lingered nearby when Marshall appeared in the hallway, eyes soft. Their hands brushed, a quiet spark in the dim light, a nod to their still growing partnership.

"You're unstoppable," Marshall said, voice low.

Morgan smiled, their touch fleeting but enough, the team's support and Marshall's presence a foundation for the road ahead.

CHAPTER TWELVE

Morgan

Morgan leaned against a gym bench, the clang of weights and sharp scent of sweat filling the air, a familiar haven amidst the storm brewing outside. His phone buzzed with a call from Gary, the screen's glow harsh in the dim gym light.

"One sponsor's waffling," Gary said, voice steady but edged with frustration. "Image concerns, they claim. Say the announcement's got them spooked. But don't worry, kiddo, I'm locking in your contract. They'll come around or we'll find better."

The words hit like a check to the boards, echoing Morgan's old fear that being openly gay could cost him his career, a shadow that lingered despite his public stand. His chest tightened, but he nodded, wiping sweat from his brow. "Thanks, Gary. I'm not backing down."

"No, we're not, kiddo. I'm just keeping you up-to-date."

When the call disconnected, he attacked the weights with ferocity, the barbell's clatter a defiant rhythm. Each rep was a proof of worth, his muscles burning as he pushed harder, determined to show the sponsors, the fans, the world that he was still a Dingo, a champion.

In the gym's mirrored wall, Morgan caught his reflection. He studied himself for a second. He was a top-condition professional hockey player claiming his place in the game and in the world. Past weaknesses didn't matter anymore, were not even worth a thought. The team's adoption of the brightly colored tape flashed in his mind, their loyalty standing between him and the rest of the world. He racked the weights, the metallic thud settling his nerves, and headed to the locker room for a well-deserved shower, resolve burning brighter. He was ready to prove his value on the ice.

***

Marshall

Marshall stood in the management box. The rink below was alive with the team's morning skate, blades hissing and pucks clacking. His clipboard held notes from Coach Matheson on ice line adjustments, but his focus drifted to the media calls piling up, scrutiny over Morgan's coming-out intensifying. As GM, thus far he'd fielded the questions with a practiced calm, pushing the league's diversity initiatives, including the newly adopted anti-harassment policies and a variety of inclusion programs. He was surprised how steady his voice stayed despite the pressure. *Their pressure and my anger.* Not every call had been supportive, and depending on their position in the world of hockey, he couldn't always correct some of their casual slurs. Morgan's courage drove him to try anyway.

"Oakson's a leader," he told a reporter over the phone, deflecting criticism. "His truth strengthens our team, our game." Hanging up, he watched Morgan skate, weaving through a drill with Thompson, their chemistry a bright spot on the ice.

Marshall's heart tugged, everything about their burgeoning relationship a delicate balance. His feelings for Morgan had only grown stronger. Marshall had started thinking about what might come next for him. If he was no longer GM of Morgan's team, then they could ignore the need to stay professional. He thought of his sister, her quiet strength during her attempts to reclaim her life, and vowed to support Morgan the same way, without crossing lines. *Can I support him the way he needs? I failed Dottie. And now I still can't face her headstone.*

He shook his head, turning away from the ongoing practice. *Focus on the here and now.*

Post-skate, Marshall caught Morgan by the tunnel, their eyes meeting briefly. "You and Thompson are killing it out there," he said, voice low, a smile tugging at his lips.

Morgan nodded, a flicker of warmth passing between them, but Marshall kept his distance, hands in pockets, his public restraint emphasizing a silent promise. The chill kept him centered, his advocacy and their vow intertwined, a foundation for Morgan's fight and the potential for their shared future.

Later, he arrived home to find Morgan in what he'd begun mentally calling their apartment. Seated on the couch, slouching back, e-reader in hand, and legs sprawled over the cushions, Morgan looked up with a soft smile.

"Welcome home," he said, and the breath caught in Marshall's chest.

"Home," he echoed. "I like coming home and finding you here. I wish we could not worry about the rest of the world and just be us."

Morgan nodded. "I understand that, totally. But until we can, I'll be here at least twice a week." He stood, put his reader aside, and walked to where Marshall lingered in the foyer. "Because I can't go too long without this." He stopped with scarcely an inch between their chests, and Marshall sucked in a breath of air that was scented with everything that was Morgan.

Marshall tilted his head one direction at the same instant that Morgan tilted the same way. They both laughed, and Marshall cupped his palm around the hinge of Morgan's jaw, pulling him closer and reangling their heads for the first kiss.

Hot and wet, his teeth scraping along Morgan's five-o'clock shadow, Marshall worked his way down

Morgan's neck and back up, placing soft, open-mouthed kisses along every inch of skin.

"Yeah," Morgan whispered, the sound loud in the quiet apartment, "this is what I need."

"I'll always give you this. Always."

***

Morgan

Morgan settled into Dr. Sanchez's office for an urgent last-minute session, the teapot missing from the side table. The room's warmth worked to soften some of his tension, but the backlash from his announcement still weighed heavy.

"There are posts calling me a 'distraction,' and some so-called super-fans have questioned my focus, insinuating that I'm chasing boys all the time. If they only knew the reality of this life." He glared at the tips of his shoes. "It's like I'm fighting to prove I belong all over it again," he said, voice low. "I had a sponsor pull out, so that, plus all the hate online, makes me question if I can be me *and* a hockey player."

Dr. Sanchez's eyes were calm, voice soothing. "Yes, but you need to understand that you're already doing it, Morgan. You're out, playing, and leading by example. The best example of strength. The backlash is noise, not truth. Your identity as a gay man, a hockey player, and even a domestic violence survivor can now be integrated, and you'll be the stronger for it." She paused with a hum. "Let me challenge you. What's one thing you're proud of right now?"

Morgan paused. "The charity game, raising all that money for queer and disadvantaged kids. Seeing the team with the Pride stuff, and that most of the fans were cheering. And scoring. Every point feels like a finger in the face of each person saying I no longer belong. I felt whole." The memory of the crowd's roar steadied him, a contrast to the fear that once defined him.

"That's your power," Dr. Sanchez said. "Hold onto that."

The session ended, and Morgan left, encouraged, ready for the next game, the tape waiting on his stick now a symbol of his fight.

Back at their apartment, he texted Marshall. *I'm shaky but okay. Thanks for being there.*

The words were simple, but the act felt like a step forward, his confidence growing, the ice calling him to prove he belonged.

CHAPTER THIRTEEN

Morgan

Morgan sat on the locker room bench, the air in the unfamiliar locker room thick with the ever-present mix of sweat and determination. His stick was freshly wrapped with rainbow Pride tape that gleamed under the fluorescent lights.

The Dingoes were set to face the Narwhals in what Morgan saw as a high-stakes game, a chance to prove his worth after the sponsor hesitancy and social media backlash. He traced the tape's vibrant colors, a symbol of his public coming-out. The weight of fear, which had once been a suffocating cage under Burke's control, was now replaced by liberation. He felt lighter. The press conference's truth had revealed a milestone that freed him to play as his whole self.

Jake sprawled beside him with a grin. "Looking sharp, Oakson. Narwhals won't know what hit 'em."

Riley, sitting nearby, chuckled. "Yeah, man, you're gonna light it up. I think the Pride tape's got extra magic."

Their banter, warm and easy, wrapped around Morgan like a shield, their loyalty a constant since he first shared his truth. He laughed, the sound genuine and a little wild. "Magic, huh? Let's see if it scores."

The locker room's clatter, sticks clicking, teammates joking, settled him, his focus sharpening as he laced his skates, ready to show the world not just that he belonged, but that this was where he was meant to be.

The Narwhals' arena pulsed with energy, the crowd's roar a tidal wave as the puck dropped, ice spraying under blades in a frenetic choreography that could be called *Knives on Ice*. Morgan skated with purpose, the blade of his stick catching the bright lights, a vivid streak of color against the white ice.

The game was tied 2-2 late in the third, the scoreboard's glare adding pressure, but Morgan's mind was clear, his body moving with the confidence of a man who'd faced his fears and won. The Narwhals pressed hard, their sticks slashing, but Morgan danced through, his focus honed.

Thompson snagged a loose puck along the boards, his lanky frame weaving past a defender with a quick deke. He fired a saucer pass across the ice, the puck landing perfectly on Morgan's tape. Morgan cycled down the boards, keeping his stickhandling tight. He flipped the puck to Jake, who took off like a man on fire, ice shavings flying as he split two Narwhals, their checks grazing his pads.

The crowd's roar faded to a hum, Morgan's world narrowing to the goalie's crouch, glove high. He watched as Jake snapped a wrist shot that went just underneath the goalie's pads, the puck rocketing through the five hole, the net responding with a solid thrum of the twine. The arena erupted with screams and cheers.

Teammates mobbed Jake, including him. In the mix, he felt Thompson's glove thumping his back, Jake's helmet clunking against his.

"That pass was meant to be!" Thompson shouted, grinning.

Morgan pumped his fist, the goal his team's defiance of every doubt, every post questioning his place. The ice felt like home, his truth and talent intertwined, the crowd's cheers a boon to his confidence.

****

Post game, he was shocked at how the rink still buzzed with celebration. Narwhal fans were crowding the boards, waving rainbow flags that fluttered like bursts of color against the arena's white walls. The Dingoes, still in their game gear, mingled with supporters wearing jerseys from the other team. Morgan had never seen anything like it. He even signed the back of a kid's Narwhals jersey, the marker's squeak mixing with the crowd's murmur. His teammates flanked him the whole time, acting like they were the security guys Gary had hired. He was doubly safe. On one side he had Jake tossing a puck to a fan, and on the other, there was Riley, shaking hands with a youth group leader. Their presence more than just a nod to the inclusion cause they'd championed together.

At a team huddle by the bench, Morgan faced his teammates, heart full. "You guys made this possible," he said, voice thick but steady. "The tape, the support. It's why I'm still here. *You're* why I'm still here, out and playing."

Jake clapped his shoulder, and he glanced around to see Riley and Thompson nodding, saying in unison, "Dingoes stick together, man." The men's laughter rang out, an echo of the loyalty that had carried him through his darkest moments.

As the crowd thinned, Morgan glanced to the stands, catching Marshall's eye. The GM stood quietly, arms folded across his chest. His smile was warm and proud. Their gaze held, a spark of connection that warmed Morgan's chest, a silent confirmation of their shared moments. The lights would eventually dim, but the glow of the team's support and Marshall's presence remained, making Morgan feel truly at home, ready for the road ahead.

***

Marshall

The apartment was quiet the way only a Sunday morning in late October can be, city sounds muffled by fog and the hush of two men who had nowhere to be.

Rain tapped the tall windows like a patient lover, and the bedside clock read 9:17 when Marshall finally stirred. Morgan was already awake, curled against his side, head on Marshall's shoulder, one leg thrown over his thigh. The sheet had slipped to their waists; Morgan traced idle circles through the speckled hair on Marshall's chest, following the line of an old scar that curved under his ribs.

"Morning," Morgan murmured, voice sleep roughened. He pressed a kiss to the scar, then another higher, working his way up Marshall's sternum with the unhurried devotion of someone who had already memorized every inch.

Marshall hummed, eyes still closed, hand settling on the small of Morgan's back. "Thought you'd sleep 'til noon."

"Couldn't," Morgan said. "Kept dreaming about your mouth." He nipped Marshall's collarbone, soothed it with his tongue. "Woke up hard."

Marshall's laugh rumbled under Morgan's cheek as he rested on his chest. "Join the club."

They stayed like that for a long while, breathing in tandem, the rain a soft percussion. Morgan's cock lay heavy against Marshall's hip, half interested; Marshall's own pressed upward against the groove of Morgan's thigh, thick and slow to wake. Neither moved to do anything about it. Not yet.

Eventually Morgan lifted his head. "Coffee?"

Marshall cracked an eye. "You're volunteering to leave this bed?"

Morgan grinned, small and wicked. "Only if you promise to stay warm for me."

He slid out from under the sheet, gloriously naked, and padded to the kitchen. Marshall watched the flex of his ass, the long line of his back, the way his hair stuck up in sleepy tufts. The apartment smelled of them—sex and sleep and the anticipation of love that came with their time together. Morgan returned minutes later with two mugs, steam curling like incense. He handed one to Marshall, then crawled back in, careful not to spill.

They drank propped against the headboard, shoulders touching, legs tangled under the quilt. Morgan's foot found Marshall's calf and stayed there. When the mugs were empty, Morgan set them on the nightstand and turned, straddling Marshall's lap without ceremony. The sheet pooled around Morgan's ass, and his cock bobbed between them, fully hard now, flushed and curving towards his belly.

"Hi," Morgan said, soft.

"Hi, yourself."

Marshall's hands settled on Morgan's hips, thumbs stroking the sharp jut of bone. Morgan leaned in and kissed him slow, coffee breath and all, until Marshall was hard beneath him, the head of his cock nudging Morgan's balls.

They rocked like that, lazy friction, mouths fused. Morgan's hands framed Marshall's face, fingers threading through his beard, tugging gently. Marshall's palms slid up Morgan's back, mapping spine and shoulder blades, the faint ridges of old hurts. When Morgan pulled back, his lips were swollen, eyes dark.

"Want you," he said. "All morning. All day. Want to take my time."

Marshall's answer was a low growl as he rolled his hips up. "Then take it."

Morgan reached for the nightstand drawer, slow, deliberate. Condom and lube, both within arm's reach because they'd learned to keep hope close. He set them on the pillow, then kissed Marshall again, deeper, licking into his mouth, each caress filthy and lush. Marshall's hands moved to Morgan's ass, spreading him gently, thumbs brushing the soft skin behind his balls. Morgan shivered, broke the kiss to mouth along Marshall's jaw, down his throat, sucking a mark just above his collarbone.

"Love how you taste," Morgan whispered. "Salt and pine and you."

He worked lower, torturing Marshall's nipples, the slope of his belly, the trail of hair that led to his cock.

Marshall's breath paused when Morgan nosed along the length of him, inhaling like the scent fed his soul. But Morgan didn't take him into his mouth. Not yet. Instead he licked a stripe up the underside, swirled around the head, then blew cool air across the wet skin.

Marshall's hips jerked. "Tease," he accused, voice filled with gravel.

Morgan's laugh was warm against his thigh. "We've got hours."

He proved it. Minutes blurred into a slow worship of Morgan's tongue tracing every vein, his fingers rolling Marshall's balls gently, the slick sound of his palm working the crown, thumb pressing just under the head until Marshall was leaking steadily. When Morgan finally took him in, it was shallow, hot, and maddening, never deep enough, pulling off every couple of minutes to kiss the tip, to murmur praise against the slick skin.

Marshall's hands fisted in the sheets. "Morgan. God, your mouth."

"Shh." Morgan crawled back up, kissing him so Marshall tasted himself. "Let me."

He gripped Marshall's thighs, and in a show of strength, tugged Marshall down onto his back in the bed, knees spread wide. Morgan knelt between his legs, eyes locked on Marshall's as he rolled the condom down his own cock. Every movement was slow and deliberate as he let Marshall watch every inch disappear under latex. The lube came next, warmed between Morgan's palms before he slicked himself with obscene sounds that made Marshall's hole clench in anticipation.

Morgan leaned over him, one hand braced beside Marshall's head, the other guiding his cock to Marshall's entrance. He didn't push in. Just rested there, both blessed pressure and a steadfast promise, kissing Marshall soft and slow, leaving him trembling with need.

"Tell me," Morgan whispered.

Marshall's legs wrapped around his waist, heels digging into the small of Morgan's back. "Want you inside me. Slow. Want to feel every second."

Morgan's eyes fluttered shut. He pressed forwards with a steady, relentless pace until the head breached the ring of muscle. Marshall exhaled, long and shaky, forcing himself to relax. Morgan paused, forehead against Marshall's, breathing through the tightness.

"Okay?" he asked.

"Very okay." Marshall nodded, hands sliding down to grip Morgan's ass, pulling him deeper. Inch by inch, Morgan sank in, until his hips met Marshall's, and they both groaned at the stretch, the perfect fit. Morgan stilled, buried to the hilt, letting Marshall adjust.

"Fuck," Marshall breathed. "You're—Christ, you're so deep."

Morgan's laugh was shaky. He pulled out slow, then slid back in, setting a languid rhythm that had the headboard tapping the wall in gentle counterpoint to the rain. Marshall's cock lay trapped between them, leaking onto his belly with every thrust. Morgan angled his hips, searching, until Marshall arched with a broken sound.

"There," Marshall gasped. "Right there. Oh, please, Morgan."

Morgan obliged, rolling his hips to hit that spot again and again, every arch of his back slow and devastating. Sweat bloomed between them, the scent joining the fragrance of coffee and rain already permeating the room. Morgan found Marshall's cock and began stroking in time with his thrusts, swiping his thumb over the slit on every upstroke. Marshall's head thrashed on the pillow, beard scraping the sheets.

"Close," he warned on a low groan.

"Not yet," Morgan said, voice strained.

He slowed, almost stopping, until Marshall was whining, hips chasing friction. Then Morgan sped up again, relentless, until Marshall finally came with a guttural groan, striping his chest and Morgan's fist. Morgan fucked him through it, drawing out every pulse, until Marshall was trembling, oversensitive.

Morgan pulled out carefully, tied off the condom, and dropped it in the bedside bin. He wasn't finished. He slicked his hand again, wrapped it around his own cock, stroking fast and rough while Marshall watched, pupils blown.

"Come on me," Marshall said, voice wrecked and velvet. "Want to feel it."

Morgan's rhythm faltered. He braced one hand on the headboard, the other flying over his cock until he came with a choked cry, painting Marshall's chest and belly in thick ropes that mingled with Marshall's release. He collapsed forward, catching himself on his elbows, kissing Marshall tenderly.

They dozed, sticky and sated, while the rain played a lullaby. When Marshall woke again, the clock read 11:43. Morgan was tracing patterns through the mess on his chest, connecting the dots of come with a lazy finger.

"Hungry?" Morgan asked.

"For you," Marshall said, rolling them so Morgan was beneath him. He kissed down Morgan's body, licking a stripe through the still drying come, then lower, taking Morgan's soft cock into his mouth. Morgan hissed, hips jerking, already half hard again.

Marshall worked him slow, using a mix of tongue and lips and the gentle scrape of teeth, until Morgan was fully erect and leaking against his tongue. He pulled off, crawled up to kiss Morgan, sharing the taste. Morgan's legs fell open, inviting.

"Again?" Marshall asked, voice rough with wonder.

Morgan nodded, reaching for a fresh condom. "Want to ride you this time."

Marshall lay back, letting Morgan roll the latex down his cock with reverent hands. More lube, warmed between Morgan's palms, slicking Marshall until he shone. Morgan straddled him, knees wide, guiding Marshall's cock to his entrance. He sank down slowly, eyes locked on Marshall's, until he was seated fully, both of them groaning at the stretch.

Morgan didn't move at first. Just sat there, impaled, hands braced on Marshall's chest, breathing through the fullness. Marshall's hands settled on his hips, thumbs stroking the V of his groin.

"Take what you need," Marshall said.

Morgan started slow with small pumps of his hips, grinding down, his cock bobbing between them with every motion. Marshall's hands slid up to pinch his nipples, rolling them gently until Morgan's rhythm faltered, head falling back. He sped up, rising and falling, the slap of skin growing louder, wetter.

Marshall watched, mesmerized. Morgan's thighs trembled, a flush spreading from his throat down on his chest. He couldn't get enough of the way Morgan's hole clenched around his cock on every downstroke. He reached between them, wrapping a hand around

Morgan's cock, stroking in time. Morgan's moans climbed higher, the sounds broken and beautiful.

"Marshall—fuck—I'm. Oh, please."

"Come for me," Marshall growled, thrusting up to meet him.

Morgan shattered, hot liquid pulsing over Marshall's fist and belly. The clench of his body dragged Marshall over the edge. He came with a roar, hips bucking, filling the condom in long pulses. Morgan rode it out, milking every drop, until they were both spent.

They stayed joined while Morgan slumped forward, forehead against Marshall's. Sweat cooled between them; the rain had softened to a drizzle. Morgan traced Marshall's beard, his lips, the laugh lines at the corners of his eyes.

"Love you," he whispered, like a secret.

Marshall kissed him softly. "Love you more."

They cleaned up eventually. Marshall went to the bathroom and got a wet washcloth, then applied it with lazy swipes. Morgan giggled like a child when his legs wouldn't hold him and Marshall had to carry him to the bathroom.

They showered together, movements slow and hands soapy, trading kisses under the spray. Marshall washed Morgan's hair, massaging his scalp until Morgan melted against him. Morgan returned the favor, fingers gentle on Marshall's scalp, then went lower, washing his back, his ass, the sensitive skin behind his balls.

Back in bed, the sheets changed with the efficiency of practice, they curled together under a fresh quilt. The clock read 2:17. Outside, the fog had lifted; sunlight slanted through the blinds, painting gold stripes across their skin.

Morgan's head rested on Marshall's chest, ear over his heart. "We should eat," he said, but made no move to leave.

Marshall's fingers carded through Morgan's damp hair. "Later."

They dozed again, waking in the late afternoon to the smell of rain-soaked city and each other. They rocked together, lazy frottage, mouths fused, until Morgan came with a soft cry, creating a new mess on Marshall's skin. Marshall followed moments later, groaning into Morgan's neck.

They lay tangled, breathing hard, the room golden with sunset. Morgan traced a finger through the come on Marshall's belly, brought it to his lips, licked it clean. Marshall watched, throat tight.

"Stay," he said—not a question.

Morgan smiled, small and fierce. "Always."

The day slipped away in increments: more kisses, more slow touches, another round in the shower that left both of them weak-kneed and laughing. They ordered pizza at dusk, ate it cross-legged on the bed, feeding each other slices, licking sauce from fingers. When the box was placed on the dresser, Morgan pushed Marshall back against the pillows, straddled his thighs, and took him in his mouth again. Each movement was slow, worshipful, until Marshall was begging, hips rolling, coming down Morgan's throat with a broken sound.

Night fell. The city lights flickered on beyond the windows, a constellation of human lives. Morgan lay sprawled across Marshall's chest, one leg hooked over his, clever fingers tracing the scar on Marshall's ribs for the hundredth time.

"Tell me something true," Morgan whispered. It had become their tradition now.

Marshall thought, thumb stroking Morgan's spine. He rephrased a truth he'd already told. "I used to think time was a debt," he said. "Something you paid back in loneliness. But today—" he pressed a kiss to Morgan's hair, "—today was interest I never want to repay."

Morgan's smile was soft against his skin. "I love you," he said, clear and steady. "Every slow second."

Marshall's arms tightened. "And I love you, every fast heartbeat."

They fell asleep like that, limbs entwined, the quilt pulled high, the rain a distant memory. Outside, the city kept moving. Inside, there was only the hush of breath, the warmth of bodies, the languorous certainty that tomorrow would bring more Sundays, more hours, more ways to get lost in each other.

CHAPTER FOURTEEN

Morgan

Morgan sat in the courtroom, the air heavy with the scent of polished wood and stale air conditioning, the judge's bench a stark focal point under buzzing fluorescent lights. The gavel's sharp crack echoed, silencing the rustle of papers and murmurs from the sparse gallery. Burke was appearing virtually, still in jail after he ambushed Morgan. But his physical absence didn't dull the weight of the moment.

Morgan's hands rested steady on his knees, no longer trembling as they had in the bad old days, when fear of Burke's fists kept him awake, heart pounding in a sparse room with a creaky bed.

The judge's voice was firm. "Burke Hammond, you are sentenced to two years for violating a valid and known restraining order, as well as extortion, with additional limits on probation."

Morgan exhaled, relief flooding him like a clean breakaway on the ice. The sentencing closed a chapter that once defined him, all those nights spent clutching the hotline talisman, expecting Burke's shadow at every turn. Now, the courtroom's sterile calm and recognition of the judge's final nod made it all felt like freedom.

Gary was beside him, and he reached over to squeeze Morgan's shoulder. "It's over, kiddo. You're free."

Morgan nodded, the weight of his past lifted as he stepped into the courthouse hall, sunlight streaming through tall windows. He thought of the short time spent in the safe house and realized he wasn't that scared man anymore. He was a Dingo, a champion, ready to live openly, unburdened by Burke's chains.

***

Morgan

Morgan slid into a vinyl booth at the suburban diner, the aroma of fresh coffee and sizzling bacon wrapping around him like only comfort food could. The jukebox hummed a soft pop tune, and checkered curtains framed the windows, casting a cozy glow over the Formica tables. Marshall sat across from him, his broad frame relaxed but eyes cautious, their public relationship still a careful dance.

With Burke's sentencing behind him, Morgan felt bold. "I want us to be open," he said, voice steady. "Public, but smart. We keep your GM role clear. I can have Gary negotiate with the owners when my extension comes up."

Marshall's smile was warm, his fingers brushing Morgan's briefly, a spark in the diner's intimacy. "I'm in, Morgan. Transparency, but we set clear boundaries. I'd like to figure out how we keep the team separated from us and give ourselves freedom and room to grow. The goal is to have no conflicts." His voice held the restraint of his professional duties, but the warmth was all for Morgan.

The brush lingered, then evolved into a full hand hold over the table, their fingers lacing tightly as the diner's bustle of clinking plates and laughter faded into the background.

Morgan squeezed, vulnerability surfacing. "Integrating this, me being gay, plus a hockey player, and now talking about a real relationship with you—it's scary, but freeing, if that make sense. Burke's gone, never to return. It's a new lease on life for me, and I want to live it."

Their hands stayed clasped, the touch grounding amid the jukebox's hum.

Marshall leaned in and whispered, "We'll make it work." He gave Morgan's hand a final squeeze and sat back. "I'd like to think about a weekend getaway soon, away from prying eyes so we can recharge and plan our steps."

Morgan nodded, the sensation of the touch lingering. The diner's cozy chaos felt like a safe space to start this new chapter. "Slow and steady, right?" he said, echoing their earlier promises. Their agreement felt like a vow as their hands brushed again, the new promise sealed in the diner's warmth.

***

Marshall

Marshall sipped his coffee, the mug's heat welcome as he met Morgan's gaze. The diner's bustle faded, their connection sharp and real. Morgan's courage, from the courtroom to this moment, was filled with a quiet strength that Marshall admired.

"We'll make it work," he said, nodding. "League will be watching, but we'll be clear, even if it takes an official relationship declaration. I'm not your coach anymore, so I'm not in charge of your ice time. You're right—we can bring in someone neutral, or even an owner, to negotiate with Gary. I can give my professional opinion, but I want to stay far from any hint of impropriety when it comes to your career. We can be professional on the ice and still be us off it." Their hands brushed again, a promise sealed in the diner's warmth.

CHAPTER FIFTEEN

Morgan

It did indeed need an official relationship declaration. The league had their lawyers work on the paperwork, and Morgan gained a whole new appreciation of what Gary did every day. Then the owners of the Dingoes surprised everybody in giving their blessing to the GM and player relationship. The only owner Morgan had met was Darryl, and he'd sat down with the two of them and listened to all the what-ifs Marshall and Morgan had come up with. He then quizzed them on each item. The only question they'd stumbled on was how long had the relationship been going on without them telling anyone.

He'd looked at Marshall and found his boyfriend looking back at him with a grin. "Foyer kiss?"

"No." Morgan shook his head. "That was last year. I liked you and everything, but we put the brakes on that attraction for months. I'd say the cabin."

"Well, definitely by the time we went to the cabin, but we wouldn't have gone there if we weren't already a couple." Marshall arched a eyebrow. "If not the first kiss, then it had to be before the final series last year. Before the Antelope."

Morgan tilted his head side to side. "I can see the argument you're making, but we weren't an item until we went to the cabin during the offseason." He could see Marshall was going to keep arguing, and Darryl looked like he might encourage the back and forth. "But there was definitely attraction from the start. After I stopped thinking of you as my coach, I fell fast."

The grin Marshall gave him was worth extending the olive branch.

Darryl clapped his hands and stood. "I hope you know that you don't need any kind of paper for me. Dingoes wouldn't be the same club without the two of you, and I'm not going to let anyone give you a reason to look for another home. In fact, I might have legal start working on extensions of both of your contracts. Siri, remind me in ten minutes to call legal to extend Davies and Oakson's contracts." He turned and headed out the door, then paused and came back.

Morgan and Marshall both stood, and when they did, their clasped hands came into view above the table. That earned them a slow grin from Darryl as he shoved his hand forward. Morgan released Marshall's hand for the shake, and then clasped Darryl's hand in turn.

"I played defense, you know?"

Morgan's eyes snapped back to the team owner. "No, sir, I didn't. Where'd you play?"

"I stopped at U12. My old man wasn't a fan." He looked around at the room filled with posters and banner replicas. "Everything in this room, he would have hated. Maybe that's why I love it so much. Morgan, you've got a gift. I love watching how well you've found your feet here. Expecting big things out of you, you know? I got the faith." He sighed. "The clinic you put on was good. My grands…granddaughter was there. I didn't know that Chloe wanted to play hockey. She's got my support, of course. I understand why she didn't tell me. So that clinic was good. Hope you've got lots more plans like that one."

Morgan grinned. "Thank you, sir. We actually do."

"Sounds good." This time when he was leaving, he got all the way to the door before he turned back again. "Keep me in the loop on that. Through Ellis, if you aren't comfortable, Davies. I like to know we're doing good in the world."

"Yes, sir," Marshall said, reaching for Morgan's hand again.

"Love you," Marshall said once they were alone.

"Love you more."

***

Morgan

Morgan joined his teammates at a bustling brunch spot, the air filled with the clatter of plates and the rich scent of maple syrup. Sunlight streamed through large windows, illuminating the long table where Jake, Riley,

Antoly, and Thompson sprawled, trading jabs and laughter over stacks of pancakes. The team's camaraderie wrapped around Morgan like a warm jersey. Their acceptance of his identity as a gay man meant he was no longer keeping secrets, but even that detail had become a celebrated part of the Dingoes' fabric. He slid into a seat, grinning as Jake passed him a coffee.

"Yo, Oakson, heard about the sentencing," Jake said, fork pausing mid-bite. "You're free, man. Time to keep owning the ice."

Riley raised his mug, smirking. "And off the ice. We heard this morning that you and Marshall are official. Dingoes got your back."

Morgan tossed a balled-up napkin, and Thompson threw it back, chuckling. "Yeah, just don't make us skate laps for your PDA."

Morgan laughed, the sound free and light, his heart full. "You guys make this easy," he said, voice thick. "Couldn't do it without you."

The guys' cheerful toasts had coffee mugs clinking, and he caught sight of Thompson's mock salute. It all cemented his place in a home he'd fought for.

As brunch wound down, Morgan stepped outside to meet Marshall, who'd planned on joining them for coffee. In the parking lot, under the curious eyes of passing people, Morgan took Marshall's hand, a bold, public step. Their fingers laced together, the touch warm, a declaration of their relationship. Morgan felt no fear, only pride, his team and love a foundation for the future.

CHAPTER SIXTEEN

Morgan

Morgan flew across the Dingoes' home rink, the ice a smooth canvas under his blades, the puck's sharp clack against his stick a rhythm of pure confidence. He deftly shoved the puck onto Thompson's stick, grinning wide around his mouthguard when the Narwhals defensemen missed the exchange, giving Thompson a chance to really stretch his legs.

The crowd's roar intensified, a tidal wave of navy-and-gold jerseys holding up banners as the Dingoes led the Narwhals 3-1 in the third period, their league-leading record a testament to their grit.

Morgan's tape gleamed under the lights, a badge of his journey from the broken man cowering under Burke's fists to the champion he was now—out, proud, and unstoppable. His heart sprinted and skipped a beat, not with fear but with exhilaration, each stride a defiance of his past.

He snagged a pass from Thompson, their chemistry electric, and deked past a Narwhals defender, ice spraying in his wake. He got the puck to Antoly just as the goalie lunged, but Antoly's snapshot found the top corner, the net rippling as the arena erupted. Fans chanted "Ding-oes! Ding-oes!" and Jake slammed into him with a jubilant hug.

"You're a beast, man!" Jake shouted over the din.

Antoly stormed over, pressing his helmet against Morgan's for a moment. "Now we are clicking, Morgan."

He grinned, the memory of all the past fear and pain silenced, completely faded in this moment. The ice was his home, his team his family, and his truth as a gay man no longer a weight but a strength, fueling every goal, every win.

***

Marshall

Marshall sat in his GM office, the city skyline glinting through the window, paperwork stacked beside a framed photo of the Dingoes hoisting the Cup. The air smelled faintly of coffee, the drink of GM champions. He was meeting with Ellis, her laptop open to a new proposal for a league-wide LGBTQ+ initiative—a youth mentorship program inspired by Morgan's courage. The tape, jerseys, charity game, and Morgan's public stand had all combined to spark something bigger, and Marshall was proud of them both, but it was tempered by the responsibility of his role.

"We're talking mentors for queer kids, rink access, scholarships," Ellis said, her pen tapping the desk. "Your push for anti-harassment policies set the stage. Morgan's story is at the heart of it."

Marshall nodded, his clipboard scribbled over with notes. They already had corporate sponsors and proposed rink schedules from most of the teams. "Let's make it real," he said, voice steady. "Kids need to see they belong, like Morgan does now."

The meeting wrapped, and Marshall leaned back, gazing at the team photo, Morgan's grin at its center. His advocacy was personal, tied to their bond, but professional, too, a balance he'd learned to navigate. The initiative was a legacy, not just for Morgan but for every player who'd ever felt like hiding. Marshall's resolve hardened. His office had become a hub of change, the future of hockey brighter because of it.

***

Morgan

Morgan glided across the rink after hours, the dim lights casting a soft glow over the arena, its quiet hum a stark contrast to game nights. Marshall skated beside him, their blades carving lazy arcs, a callback to their cautious rink-side moment months ago. The air was crisp, their breaths fogging as they stopped at center ice, the silence intimate.

"I know it's a ways out, but do you have any offseason plans?" Morgan asked, his voice light but hopeful. "I'm thinking travel. Like maybe Europe. Try and see some international games, and maybe just find a quiet place and stay there for a while."

Marshall's smile was warm, his hand brushing Morgan's, a spark that felt like home. "I'm in. Maybe we add advocacy and talk to youth programs abroad. Keep pushing." The words held promise, their relationship now public but still careful, a balance of love and duty.

Morgan reached up to pull Marshall down, and their lips met in a soft caress. The kiss lingered, a seal on their love and Morgan's freedom.

Playful energy sparked through him, and Morgan tugged Marshall into a gentle chase, gliding backward with a grin as Marshall matched him stride for stride, still trying to catch up. They ended up against the boards, breathless, bodies pressed close. The kiss reignited, deeper now, Morgan's fingers threading into Marshall's hair, Marshall's tracing the faded scar on Morgan's arm from a long-ago hit, symbolic of his journey. "We've come so far," Marshall murmured against his lips, a neck kiss following, soft and teasing.

Morgan pulled back, grinning, the future open. Maybe they'd do international tours, advocacy battles, possibly look for a global spotlight. *Or maybe we'll just be ourselves, Marshall and Morgan.* "We've got this," he said, squeezing Marshall's hand.

As they skated off, Morgan felt the ice's promise, their love and his truth a beacon for whatever lay ahead.

The End

ABOUT THE AUTHOR

Raised in the south, MariaLisa learned about the magic of books at an early age. Every summer, she would spend hours in the local library, devouring books of every genre. Self-described as a book-a-holic, she says "I've always loved to read, but then I discovered writing, and found I adored that, too. For reading...if nothing else is available, I've been known to read the back of the cereal box."

Also by MariaLisa deMora

Shatter the Ice Series

In the ruthless world of professional hockey, where vulnerability can end a career in a heartbeat, two men risk everything for a love that could either save them—or destroy them.

Morgan Oakson is the league's quiet defenseman: talented, stoic, and hiding a dangerous secret. Trapped in an abusive relationship with his controlling boyfriend, he's one brutal hit away from breaking. When a desperate 911 call brings his openly gay coach, Marshall Davies, into his life, Morgan is given one chance to escape the violence behind closed doors.

What begins as survival becomes something deeper. Through the adrenaline of chasing the Cup, the raw work of healing old wounds, and the courage to live openly, Morgan and Marshall build a love strong enough to face grief, public scrutiny, and new threats. Together they create change— mentoring the next generation, launching a #HockeyForAll movement, and proving that the hardest fights aren't always on the ice.

Raw, emotional, and unapologetically queer, the Shatter the Ice trilogy is a sweeping hurt/comfort sports romance that follows one couple's journey from darkness to triumph:

- ***Playing for Keeps*** *– The gripping escape*

- ***One More Face-Off*** *– The hard work of healing*

- ***Beyond the Boards*** *– The legacy they build together*

Heart-pounding hockey action, deep emotional stakes, and a love that refuses to stay hidden. Perfect for fans of hurt/comfort, found family, and stories where love wins the ultimate victory.

Grab your jersey, wrap your stick in Pride tape, and experience the complete Shatter the Ice series—where the bravest plays happen off the ice.

MariaLisa deMora

Sunnybrook Cottage Daycare Series

In the charming Pacific Northwest town of Willow Creek, Sunnybrook Cottage Daycare is more than a haven of giggles, glitter, and rainbow doors—it's a sanctuary where innocence meets intrigue. *Wall Street Journal* and *USA Today* bestselling author MariaLisa deMora weaves heartwarming cozy mysteries around Theresa Daye-Reed, devoted daycare owner, foster (and soon adoptive) mom to Emily, fiancé (and then wife) to charming librarian Alex, and guardian of pint-sized dreamers.

From **Daycare Dangers** (Book 1), where cryptic kid quips expose corporate murder and family secrets, to **Daycare Shadows** (Book 2), where haunting drawings reveal trauma and hidden estates, to **Daycare Whispers** (Book 3), where faint murmurs and prophetic sketches unearth generational echoes—the series balances light suspense with profound emotional healing.

Each story celebrates found family, protector shadows, big-sister bonds, pregnancy milestones, and the power of truth to chase away darkness. With hilarious kid quips, sensory gardens, and the iconic Exit Express swing, Theresa navigates threats while nurturing her growing family and community, including the launch of Alex's bookstore, Reed Between the Lines.

Perfect for fans of heartwarming cozies with depth, these tales prove that even in whispering winds, rainbows always win. Join Theresa, Emily, Alex, and the rest of the Sunnybrook crew for stories where hugs heal, crayons conquer, and brighter futures whisper just around the corner.

Discover the series today—where every mystery ends with light.

5-Star Reviews for Daycare Dangers

"I loved the characters, the build up of tension and the wonderful children that provide such a powerful impact...."

~Lynne B

"Grab a cup of coffee, snuggle up on your couch, and settle in for a cozy mystery! This is just a good ole wholesome fantastic read. Teachers are wonderful, and when they set out to scare the monsters away, they are even better! After all, monsters are allergic to the truth!"

~Tracey

"I was highly interested in this theme of daycare, danger, and mystery. MariaLisa kept me on the edge of my seat the entire read. I was waiting for what would happen next with clenched teeth (should have read it with my mouthguard in). In many placed I shouted, "YES!". My heart pounded. I was enthralled. I had tears in my eyes as I tried to explain the story to my husband."

~Gail

MariaLisa deMora

Borderline Freaks MC

Rev Up Your Heart with the Borderline Freaks MC –
Where Brotherhood Roars Louder Than Thunder!

Strap in for a pulse-pounding ride through the
gritty, high-octane world of the Borderline Freaks
Motorcycle Club, where loyalty is forged in steel,
danger lurks around every bend, and love hits harder
than a revved-up Harley. From the acclaimed author
MariaLisa deMora comes this addictive four-book
series that blends raw MC brotherhood with scorching
romance, heartfelt redemption, and edge-of-your-
seat action.

In **Service and Sacrifice**, honor the unsung heroes of
military life as a veteran's path intersects with the
club's unbreakable bonds, reminding us that true
freedom comes at a cost – and love can heal the
deepest wounds.

Shift gears into **More Than Enough**, where a near-
fatal crash leaves one brother questioning his worth,
only to discover that the right woman can make even
the most damaged soul feel whole again.

Accelerate through **Lack of In-between**, as hidden
secrets unravel in a whirlwind of passion and peril,
drawing a resilient woman deeper into the club's
fierce embrace.

Finally, throttle wide open in **See You in Valhalla**,
facing the ultimate test of legacy when loss strikes the

heart of the club, forcing new leaders to rise from the ashes and defend what matters most.

Perfect for fans of physical drama laced with steamy, soul-stirring romance, the Borderline Freaks MC series delivers non-stop thrills, complex characters, and happily-ever-afters that will leave you craving more. Grab the complete set today and join the ride because in this club, family isn't just blood...it's everything.

With My Whole Heart Series

Dive into the heartfelt world of the *With My Whole Heart* series, where unconventional families forge unbreakable bonds through love, laughter, and life's unexpected twists. Sweet as pie and twice as delicious, these steamy romantic tales deliver guaranteed happily-ever-afters that will warm your soul and steal your breath.

In **With My Whole Heart** (Book 1), meet Jaime, a fierce single mom battling to keep her world afloat, and Connor, a man too busy for love—until fate intervenes. When Jaime becomes the surrogate for Connor's big brother, and Connor steps up as the sperm donor, sparks fly in the most complicated way. What starts as a family favor blossoms into a passionate romance, proving that true love thrives in the messiest of circumstances. Readers rave: "This book has a special place in my heart. I was pulled in from the first words to the last." With a 4.44 average rating on Goodreads, this story of unconditional love and second chances is impossible to put down.

Continue the journey in **Bet on Us** (Book 2), where Trent and Jacob's dream of building a family collides with tragedy. When Trent discovers his estranged sister's murder leaves behind a teenage nephew, Jericho—a quiet kid hiding a big secret— the couple steps in as guardians. Amid grief and revelations, Jericho finds strength in his uncles' fierce loyalty, echoing themes of acceptance and love. This sweetly complicated tale expands the beloved family from Book 1, blending romance, resilience, and hope. Earning a stellar 4.66 average rating, fans call it "a lover of romance and heartbreaking stories" must-read.

Perfect for fans of emotional contemporary romance with LGBTQ+ representation, found family vibes, and steamy connections. Whether read as standalones or together, these books remind us that love wins—every time. Grab the series today and fall in love with characters who feel like family!

5-Star Reviews for **With My Whole Heart**

"This story is such a beautiful story of love, loss, and life. Jamie has lived a hard life as a single mom of Nate who by the way is a genius! Connor lost a part of his soul, and never thought he would find love. I would recommend the heck outta this book, it is such a feel good love story,

~Kindle Reader

"I wish I could give Jaime and Connor more than 5 stars. I wish everyone who loved a sweet, hopeful love story that was slightly complicated would read this. [...] My enjoyment of this book is twofold. 1) It's not a storyline I've read before so it was fresh, and by the end, I was definitely wondering what I would do if I was in Jaime's shoes. 2) It's by a favorite author, she up until now writes exclusively MC and I HOPE this helps her to take another chance and give us something like this again."

~Megan

"This book is why I continue to read romance. Two wonderful characters who are just drawn to one another; in spite of reasons that it might not be for the best that they become a couple. Throw in one heck of a wonderful young boy and a family is created. [...] WITH MY WHOLE HEART is the best among a group so filled to the brim. It's not always easy to find that diamond in the rough, and if you are looking for a warm heart, drama, very little angst, lots of soul, and flawless writing........look no further."

~C Marie

5-Star Reviews for Bet On Us

1. Review by Anonymous (October 28, 2019)

"This book definitely deserves way more than five stars. The absolute love and devotion between Trent and Jake was just beautiful. Watching their love expand to include their nephew was just profound. They never even hesitated, even though they didn't know he existed. [...] Jericho was a fifteen year old boy who had endured constant abuse from his step father while his mother did little to stop it, though she didn't know about it all. [...] His story is heart rendering and left me in tears on several occasions. The grief he endured and the anger he felt towards his mother was handled perfectly, including the unanswered questions as many endure."

~Anonymous

"This is a story of family and acceptance as much as it is a romance. [...] There are really so many layers to this story that I don't know where go with this review. There is the love between Trent and Jacob, the development of their family, Jericho's coming out and finding acceptance where he was accustomed to scorn, his learning what family should be, him finding his way in his new life and finally finding the love he is so deserving of. I highly recommend this book."

~Kat

"Straight to my heart. I swear I felt it grow two sizes as I read Bet On Us. [...] MariaLisa takes us on a whirlwind ride with Trent and Jacob and their new family member, Jericho, Trent's nephew he knew nothing of until he's faced with being his only living relative after his sister dies. [...] Love, without borders, zero conditions, and in amounts that are unfathomable to Jericho are his future. [...] A story about family, even when they're so new and fresh, love without conditions, life lessons and just finding their way. Heartbreaking and beautiful."

~Megan

ADDITIONAL SERIES AND BOOKS

Please note that books in a series frequently feature characters from additional books within that series. If series books are read out of order, readers will twig to spoilers for the other books, so going back to read the skipped titles won't have the same angsty reveals.

Rebel Wayfarers MC series:

Mica, #1
A Sweet & Merry Christmas, #1.5
Slate, #2
Bear, #3
Jase, #4
Gunny, #5
Mason, #6
Hoss, #7
Harddrive Holidays, #7.5
Duck, #8
Biker Chick Campout, #8.5
Watcher, #9
A Kiss to Keep You, #9.25
Gun Totin' Annie, #9.5
Secret Santa, #9.75
Bones, #10
Gunny's Pups, #10.25
Never Settle, #10.5
Not Even A Mouse, #10.75
Fury, #11
Christmas Doings, #11.25
Gypsy's Lady, #11.5
Cassie, #12
Road Runner's Ride, #12.5

Occupy Yourself band series:

Born Into Trouble, #1
Grace In Motion, #2
What They Say, #3 (TBD)

Neither This, Nor That MC series:

This Is the Route Of Twisted Pain, #1
Treading the Traitor's Path: Out Bad, #2
Shelter My Heart, #3
Trapped by Fate on Reckless Roads, #4
Tarnished Lies and Dead Ends, #5

Rebel Wayfarers crossover stories:

Going Down Easy
No Man's Land
In Search of Solace
Puppy Love
Steel and Swagger

Mayhan Bucklers MC series:

Most Rikki-Tik, #1
Mad Minute, #2
Pucker Factor, #3
Boocoo Dinky Dau, #4

MariaLisa deMora

Borderline Freaks MC series:

Service and Sacrifice, #1
More Than Enough, #2
Lack of Inbetween, #3
See You in Valhalla, #4

Alace Sweets series:

Alace Sweets, #1
Seeking Worthy Pursuits, #2
Embarrassment of Monsters, #3
All the Broken Rules, #4

With My Whole Heart series:

With My Whole Heart, #1
Bet On Us, #2

If You Could Change One Thing:
Tangled Fates Stories

There Are Limits, #1
Rules Are Rules, #2
The Gray Zone, #3

Other Books:

Outlaw Heartstrings
Sidetracked Love
Only For You
Hard Focus
Salvaged Parts
Spark of the Lock
Dirty Bitches MC: Season 3

More information available at **mldemora.com**.

www.ingramcontent.com/pod-product-compliance
Lightning Source LLC
Chambersburg PA
CBHW060919140726
47996CB00001B/309